A DREAM BETWEEN TWO RIVERS

HIGH PRAISE FOR *A DREAM BETWEEN TWO RIVERS*

"*A Dream Between Two Rivers: Stories of Liminality* is a precious gem all its own. Folk tales, experimental literature, speculative fiction, and mythology whether invented or neoclassical, all play together here gorgeously. The ghosts of Gabriel García Márquez, José Donoso, Leonora Carrington, and Octavia Butler haunt this potent collection by an author of boundless imaginative gifts. Imagine a poet and painter in another dimension possessed by fever dreams and trying to tell our stories, and that will bring you only somewhere close to the magic of KL Pereira." **—POROCHISTA KHAKPOUR, author of** *Sons & Other Flammable Objects, The Last Illusion,* **and** *Sick*

"KL Pereira's *A Dream Between Two Rivers* is a wonderfully dark, evocative, mischievous collection. Pereira expertly reinvents familiar favorites and prods at the boundaries of genre with a unique, eloquent voice. With wit and compassion *A Dream Between Two Rivers* unflinchingly explores what it means to be human." **—PAUL TREMBLAY, author of** *A Head Full of Ghosts* **and** *Disappearance at Devil's Rock*

"Take a soaring imagination, dazzling prose, and a merciless eye for truth. Mix with an ability to explode our acceptable truth and you'll have the stories of KL Pereira, a writer who spins tales that veer from velvet to etched in acid on glass and back again. Pereira's talent and poetry leap off the pages of *A Dream Between Two Rivers.*"
—RANDY SUSAN MEYERS, international bestselling author of *Widow of Wall Street*

"Once this collection gripped me in its maw, it was impossible to put down and haunted my dreams for days after I was done reading. Each of Pereira's stories is stranger than the last and, through their explorations of identity, desire, and purpose, expose some deep truths about us as individuals. Lyrical, visceral, and taut, *A Dream Between Two Rivers* is a master work of a fever dream."   —LANE JACOBSON,
Flyleaf Books (Chapel Hill, NC)

"*A Dream Between Two Rivers* is a series of twenty-seven virtuosic performances from a writer to watch. KL Pereira's wild yet self-contained fictions succeed in both the short and the short-short form. She's razor-sharp about the mysteries of the heart, and her stories have a refreshingly global and historical scope. The set of second-person addresses in *A Dream . . .*, especially, amaze. Nowhere else, recently, have I read a 'you' as versatile as Pereira's. An eclectic and exciting collection from a promising new press."   —JOHN FRANCISCONI,
Bank Square Books (Mystic, CT)

A DREAM
BETWEEN
TWO RIVERS

STORIES OF LIMINALITY

KL PEREIRA

CUTLASS PRESS

The Publishing Arm of Papercuts J.P

Boston, Massachusetts

Published by Cutlass Press
The Publishing Arm of Papercuts J.P.
5 Green Street
Boston, Massachusetts 02130

Cover design and part opener illustrations by Stacey Dyer
Interior design by Matt Tanner
Illustrations © by Anna Cassell www.annamcassell.com

ISBN: 9780692864685

First Edition

Printed in the United States of America

For my father, my partner in crime and cryptozoology

"I don't want to choose between light or dark. I think there is a third choice. It includes light and dark but is not limited to either. It's more and more."

—Selah Saterstrom, *The Meat and Spirit Plan*

CONTENTS

THE LONELINESS

THE DARK VALLEY OF YOUR LUNGS

The first time you saw her, she was getting change from the machine in the lavandería; copper and nickel clacked against her metal palms, a rain of clicks pricking your eardrums. She was just as grotesque as your sister said: silvery fingers stiff as stone, jointless and smooth, unable to pluck the money from the open mouth of the change-maker. She struggled to scoop the coins into the stiff basket of her hands but you wouldn't help her. You were too busy praying to Saint Lucy to take away your voice for good this time.

After your father's death, you couldn't speak; your throat was dry and not even startled bird sounds flew from it. When you were finally able to nod for yes and shake for no, your mother sent you back to school because what else could she do with you?

It was autumn and the neighbor's cat was twining around your legs and you bent and ran your short brown fingers down its back and up its tail and what could you do but sigh at the feeling of soft silky fur? You hadn't meant to. Until that moment, you hadn't even known that you could make that airy rumble in your throat. The cat stumbled then, looked at you and then behind you with eyes so dilated there was almost no green left in them and then limped away under the front bush. It was strange, but then people had been running from you since your father died, the tiny mute girl who witnessed it all.

When you came back from school that afternoon, your neighbor was looking and looking but never found her cat. You cried into the orange carpet beneath your bed because you loved cats and had hoped you were not such a bad girl, that the first time, the time with your father, was just an accident. You started to breathe long and even and slept with your hands around your neck so no sounds would come out while you were dreaming.

You were doing so well, until the day the boy fell over. You hadn't known your tongue started to work again, could push the airy hum that you kept pressed down in your chest into stubborn syllables, until the boy decided to stab you in the cheek with a pencil. You were all the way at the back of the room and the boy, who was only as cruel as children can be, turned to you and jabbed the yellow stick into the softest part of your face. The jagged point of the lead ripped your skin and made it burn. His eyes dared you to tell and so help you, your voice swept from the dark valley of your lungs, not loud but fast and you couldn't have stopped it. What you whispered was unintelligible but terrible enough and you'll never forget the tremble of his eyes and the convulsing of his lips or the blood that pooled after his head hit the floor.

You wrote his mother that you were sorry but she never wrote you back and your ma didn't send you to school after that. Your ma asked your abuela, who was still alive back then, what to do with you and Abuela said you must pray to the Virgin but that hasn't gotten you anywhere. So you pray to Saint Lucy and when you're supposed to be kneeling on the hard wooden floor of the confessional or doing penance by cleaning houses while everyone is doing laundry or shopping or work and making very sure you do not open your mouth, you walk around the town pretending you are the only one alive. Because you could be.

You see her the second time outside of the church. Your ma and your tías have told your sister the woman was exiled here. They are all afraid of her, disgusted by her. How could she let a man do that to her? She's too calm and unashamed, walking with her head high in crowds, nodding to the matriarchs of the town. She doesn't offer apologies when she catches children, or even adults, staring at her hands, her feet. You never see her slinking out from behind the dark walnut of the confessional, or pressing her forehead to the polished shoulders of the pew in front of her, or taking the Communion. You wonder if she's even Catholic. You are, just like everyone else you know.

Saint Lucy is your favorite saint because you can talk to her in your full voice and she doesn't mind. She scared people, too. She plucked out her own eyes to stop a pagan king from adding her to his harem. When he found out she'd disfigured herself, he had her beheaded. Now she walks around where the spirit world and the people world rub against one another like cats on a new couch, her eyes held before her on a bright blue plate, eye-sockets dark caverns in her face. Even though your ma tells you to pray to Saint Jude, the patron saint of hopeless causes, you pray to Saint Lucy, the protector of those who have trouble with their eyes and throats. You pray she'll take your voice away for good, or at least steal your ma's eyes so she won't have to look at you.

Your sister says she knows for a fact that the woman with the silver hands is in the witness protection program, saw the feds parked outside her door.

How d'you know they're feds? Isn't she from China or somewhere? You scribble on a memo pad in big block letters and hold it up to your sister from across the room.

Your sister loves you, but will only let you sit with at least a room between you, in case you get excited or angry, in case you can't help it, she explained. It's not that she doesn't love you, Abuela told you once. She just fears Death.

Your sister reads the pad and just gives you a look. She watches a lot of television, all of the murder shows and detective shows and cop shows and if anyone knows feds, it is her.

Well, how do you know they were there for her? The memo pad is full so you write this on the thick back cover.

—Please, she says. Who else would they be here for?

It's true. Why would the feds come here? you wonder.

Later, you will hate yourself for it but you wonder what the woman did wrong. What she did to deserve it—being cut and sent away. Did she do something as horrible as you did?

Probably worse, you think. At least they let you stay.

∾

The third time you see the woman, she's in the produce aisle of the grocery. It is a Friday, a day when most women are at the laundromat, catching up on gossip and telenovelas while their whites and darks spin in lazy circles. Your ma and tías are probably there, too. No one shops on Fridays. You, however, have decided it's the perfect day to visit Lorenzo, your only friend, who is deaf and whom you therefore cannot hurt, in the vault of the funeraría, where they keep the bodies before they go underground. You will get kiwis for him because he has a weakness for strange fruit. Then you will sneak off and visit your abuela.

The woman is standing in front of the melons. They are round, ripe, huge as your tías' breasts, and their warm smell tells you that they are already mush inside—too soft, like the head of a new baby. But the woman doesn't seem to catch their scent. Instead she places the melons in her basket, cocks her head and moves to the nectarines, the plums, the strawberries. She must feel them to know if they are good to buy. You see her press the tip of her hard finger to their tiny fleshy bodies, one by one.

You wonder: How can she feel ripeness? Anticipate the taste on her tongue?

You feel sorry for her. You wonder: What would it be like to never know if the fruit at your lips will run juicy down your chin, or crunch dry between your teeth?

You pluck a perfectly red strawberry from its sage-green carton and with gentle pressure, you run your thumb down its seed-speckled fullness. It is perfect. Then, without flinching, but also without touching, you place it in the palm of her silver hand.

The woman looks at you and nods. She pays for the fruit, yours and hers, and follows you out of the store.

~

Later, at the café, she tells you to call her Marsha. You wonder what her real name is.

She says that her hands and feet were removed. Not cut or lopped or hacked off. For a moment, it makes you think that maybe, just maybe they were surgically separated from her body at birth, due to some kind of defect. This thought, your thought, makes you feel momentarily comforted.

Before you can begin to imagine how a baby can crawl with no hands or feet, she says:

—You are the first person to acknowledge me. Even the cashiers at the bodega look away from me, keep silent, as if their lips were as hard as my hands.

You are sitting at a dirty plastic table, drinking strong coffee, even though your mother has warned you that this will stunt your growth. You stir a pure white waterfall of sugar and a lake of cream into your cup. Marsha does not touch her coffee. And even though she is strange and broken, you somehow know that it would be impossible for you, as evil as your ma says you are (and she is probably right), to hurt her. Perhaps it is the way she looks at you, as if she has already forgiven you for whatever you might do, whatever you have done.

You decide to open your mouth because for once, someone is talking to you and is not afraid and this makes you brave. You breathe in, fill the shadowy caves of your lungs and then, slowly, let them collapse with your words.

—You'll get used to it, you whisper. They do not like anyone to be more interesting than them. My abuela used to call them the *quedadas malas*. They don't like me either. I call Death.

You don't tell her why. You don't know why, not yet. You are sure that if she sticks around town long enough, she will figure this out on her own. Her eyes are black and round as the cup of coffee between her hands. She does not reply, does not try to comfort you. She simply watches: a very still animal waiting for something to happen, a change in wind, a shift in the shadows.

—So, what are you doing here?

Impatient, your voice splashes into the air, louder than you meant it to, but she is as still as the statue of Saint Lucy you pray to every night, and for a brief but flaming second you are afraid, truly afraid, that you've killed her. That her eyes will run and her mouth will weep with saliva and you will be left, again, with the body.

Her eyes are so still, pools of oil, and her skin is the solid yellow-brown sand of the earth. And then she says:

—I've come for you.

She doesn't flinch when she says this. Something in her tone calls to you: an understanding, a kinship, something in her deep eyes and careful words makes you feel you could fall into her arms, the blanket of her compassion warming you, that you could stay there forever and not be afraid. You hold your breath until the lights in the corners of the café go flashing and blue and then you let it out. You tell her everything.

～

You are not supposed to confess your sins to anyone except the priest (the priest who will not hear you, who lets you sit in the brown dark of the confessional alone because even he fears for his life), but you do. You lay your woe at the silver feet of this woman you just met, this woman you are supposed to ignore, but who has somehow, miraculously come for you. You tell her about your father's death, when you were just a baby in his arms. How he sang to you: *mi cielo mi cielo mi cielo*, and how you, after months of trying, could finally form the sounds, say the words back to him. You loved your papa, your heaven. You did not understand when his pupils shrank and his mouth gaped and all the muscles in his face went slack and he fell on the slick lino of the kitchen floor, and when you saw the blood you called and called until you lost your voice and someone you did not know came to take him away. You tell her about your abuela, who years later believed you when you drew out for her what you'd done and who told you it was no evil but a gift, a gift she made you promise to use when she was old and suffering too much and you were the only one who could do it and so you did, just like she asked, and now, now everyone hated you, especially your mother who missed her husband and her mother, and would never ever forgive you for calling Death to take them.

You lead Marsha to the cemetery. The day to clean the graves is months away and most stones lie in neglect, covered with the dust of rotten flowers. Marsha sits at the foot of your abuela's stone and watches as you polish the statues of Guadalupe and kiss the head of your own Saint Lucy and place her with her plate of eyes in the middle of the marble, flanked by petunias and marigolds and three ripe strawberries. You've already told Marsha everything when she says:

—When I was a girl in Xi'an, I played the violin. I could make the bow and the wood sing and all who heard me swore it was more beautiful than the cries coming from the very heart of the goddess Kwan Yin. Do you know her?

You shake your head, snake your hand to the top of the gravestone and sneak a small strawberry. Since you sat on the warm earth the scent of ripeness has been stealing into your nostrils and you cannot help yourself. Your abuela would not mind.

—She is the goddess who hears all the suffering of the world and is said to give comfort. She does not flinch from death, nor from life, no matter how full of sorrow. Marsha continued, In any case, I was promised to a very wealthy, very cruel man. My father said that the man would ensure that I had the finest education, lessons from the masters of string, and entrances to the greatest orchestras in the world. I only had to obey him. It was not hard to say yes—I was very young, what did I know of marriage?

—So you were married?

Marsha looks not much older than your sister. You want to ask her if she misses her father but instead you suck the fruit into your mouth. You are not used to interrupting, to the deep ocean of your voice and the way it sounds when it is full, when it does not kill.

Marsha places her shining hands on her knees, palms up and squints at the sky.

—Yes. Yes, we were married. We were not happy. We loved different things. I loved my music and he loved having a wife, a possession.

—But how was he cruel? Did he lock you in a tower?

You think of all the fairy tales you were ever told, the stories you and Lorenzo tell each other with your hands in the dark recesses of the funeraría vaults where only the dead can hear.

—No. Listen.

Marsha's voice is strong and clear and all the stones in the cemetery shake like they are going to crack and her eyes fix on you: black and shiny and terrifying and ready to swallow you if you say another word.

—What matters is that I had a gift and he stole it away. How can I describe how creating music felt? It was more than the hum along the strings, the small brown body of the violin trembling beneath my chin; it was as if every sorrow there ever was had shaken loose from the world. I had just started my instruction at the conservatory when I became pregnant. My husband would not allow me to be a mother and a violinist. My place was by his side. He was a lonely man and the prospect of a child made him believe that he could keep me, keep us forever, objects in his collection. But how could I give up the one thing that made me who I was? So I refused.

Her words are nails piercing coffin-wood. The sparrows in the trees above stop their chittering and sit perfectly still, tiny brown stones waiting to fall from the leafless trees.

You look at her hands then, thinking that you understand.

—No, little girl. It was not simply what was taken from me that made me what I am. It was what I found after.

She raises her palms and all the light in the world streams into them. The grass, the trees, the gravestones—everything—falls colorless, simple shades of glass and shadow. Nothing moves. Not even the air. Not even your chest.

And in this place of still smoke and mirrors you start to know your gift. You close your eyes and know: you are the woman in the boat who cradles the king's head, you are the saint who sits beside the goddess of mercy, you are Death and though you are feared, you need not fear yourself.

You open your eyes and again, are in the day, the cemetery. You sit beside Marsha, the woman, the outcast, the only person you can speak to in your full voice. You will follow her, wherever it is that she takes you.

She lifts a perfectly round watermelon from her bag and with heavy, silvery hands, knocks on the jungle-green skin of the fruit. You feel the dull thump deep in your chest and before she cracks the rind you know the pink taste of sweetness, can feel it flood your mouth, your throat, your heart.

PRIPYAT

Pripyat, a city in Ukraine, was founded in 1970 to house the families of workers in the Chernobyl Nuclear Power Plant. After the explosion on April 26, 1986, Pripyat was mostly abandoned. It is now a tourist attraction.

Pripyat was a city but now Pripyat is ghosts. Long grey snouts and round glass eyes. They stomp through the flat, the glomps of their muddy boots sticking in my ears as I hide. I am meant to be asleep. Or maybe gone. The clock on the wall says 3 o'clock, time for Baba to begin the roast—carrots, turnips, a butt of meat—the flesh golden, electric heat sucking pink juices from the skin. Baba once told stories: a dark-mouthed oven hungry for the fat arms of children who got too close, nasty, half-dead geese escaping from its greasy blackness to pull you in. Now Baba keeps her face turned from the closed lips of the stove and does not answer when I speak to her.

My ear to the outside wall, I listen closely for Pripyat and hear nothing. I slide out from behind green drapes, quiet as a cat in the forest. The grey-suited ghosts never hear me making a sound. They will not take me away.

Boba lies on the couch. He was a guard at the power plant but now he sleeps, waits—for what I do not know—shaving cream spotting his neck and the tongues of his collar. I remember when he used to shave my cheeks. "Hold very still now," he would say, one palm thick and warm against my chin. "Still as stones, Goruchka," his finger a pretend razor ready to sweep the cream away. Boba's face is stony in his sleep, like he is holding his breath.

I laugh, think of the games children make adults play. Surely soon Baba will awaken and find me a groom—if the ghosts do not find me. I didn't know to hide until the day of the explosions—the television was on and I watched other grey men tapping the tiny glass screen on every channel, saying words like evacuation, radiation, explosion, Pripyat, Pripyat, Pripyat. Boba stared hard at the ghosts, prepared himself like he was going to a wedding or a funeral, kissed my cheek, and went to sleep on the couch. Baba was already sick in the kitchen, crying and vomiting in the corner.

"Let no one inside, Goruchka. Promise me," her silver-spun hair looked almost yellow, "if anyone comes, hide." Her eyes were grey stones. "The snouted men are ghosts who take girls away, make experiments of them, feed them to monsters."

Baba had been taken from here once, to Germany. She swore that leaving home was almost certain death.

They came soon after but did not find me. I hid behind the drapes, my face tingling and red hot. Their name was painted on the chests of their suits with the other words from the television. They do not come back as often now; perhaps when they do it is only a dream, a trick—the glow of the moon so like the sick yellow of their glass eyes, shining on the television that no longer turns on.

POMPEII

The day we moved ash fell like snow on a February day, blanketing old stairs that burned under our feet, our tongues darting out, not yet knowing these white-grey crystals as toxic.

It was a neat asphyxiation: sitting behind the drawn blinds limned with the last of the sun, waiting for a slow death to find me, watching my mother scald her moist hands dry under the tap washing the dishes until they disintegrated into hot ash.

She'd tell me to watch, listen for eruptions that could spew us all into the sky—this, and other empty warnings before she left for work. Remember—she'd say, haloed by the musty light of the open door, lava pooling around her sensible shoes—no boys. And if you see the ash cloud coming toward you, run. She wiped her hands on my cheeks, traces of our melted dishes smudging my kohl-painted face.

Our Pompeii was clattered terracotta and pyroclastic urges that led to untimely demise.

Years later, revisiting my childhood city, I stood with tourists, a brochure in hand that said: "Experience the Destruction!", saw 32 skeletons fused together in an Escher-like maze of bones, in positions that seemed impossible even in agony.

I tried but couldn't recognize their faces. Did their screams live somewhere in my memory? Did I intentionally forget them?

It was only when I saw the melted stoop, the glass blasted back to sand, that I remembered the day we moved there, why we stayed, how in the other house, with the other man, my mother had held her hand over her mouth to avoid suffocation, how at this beginning, at that end, we shared a twin bed—two girls, my head buried in her chest, her hollow birth canal and accordioned ribs enclosing me, our mouths opening and closing trying to breathe.

NOT QUITE TAKEN

I.

It starts with your fingers. Even in the cool air you feel the bite of the decay chewing your skin, and you take up smoking again so that anyone who cares to notice (no one ever cares to notice) will see clouds of grey streaming from your lips and assume at least some of it was the heat of your breath meeting winter air.

"Spare a fag, love?" The woman is so time-worn than you want to ask her if maybe she hasn't just misplaced her pack somewhere in her folds of skin. You get meaner when you start dying. You've noticed that. Her grey eyes are so pale they are almost white, a heathery northern sky, and you slip her two like a silent apology.

"Ta, love." She lights both with a sure hand and begins to hum something that feels so familiar, you're sure you've heard it before, right here, on this spot. But that's not possible, is it? You've taken all the precautions.

Nevertheless, you move away, decide to walk to the next railway stop from here on out. The tune continues to drive into your brain, lightning rods stabbing behind your eyes through your commute and even into the night when you're back in the safe dark of your house.

II.

Your skin gets dry. Dry is perhaps a ridiculous word for it. It feels like someone, some unseen Egyptian undertaker is continually rubbing salt into your flesh. Once you slathered yourself with lotion, wrapped yourself in gauze chanting "Mummy, mummy, perhaps I will wake up as Boris Karloff, yes?" toward the cat, who barely acknowledges you when you're in this state. Mostly, she narrows her yellow eyes and turns her grey nose down before returning to sleep. That time she cocked her head, as if to say: "Stupid human" and hid in the closet from the smell. It came off you in waves, like your skin did soon after. You don't want to think about how you looked without your skin, kidney brown and red and moist. You can almost feel the pain now, just thinking about it. You wear loose linen and sandals while you molt. You let yourself itch, knowing that eventually, other parts of you must go. Of course, the skin always takes the longest.

III.

You start to feel sluggish in the mornings, walking to the railway station that is farthest from your house but close enough for you to get to unaided. You hate depending on others, and as your muscles begin to stiffen, you tell yourself that this time you'll push yourself a bit more each day, keep yourself limber, well-oiled like the Tin Man, dancing in a technicolor forest of poison apple trees and dogs and witches. Your joints protest as you sit down and one morning, as you sit across from a small child on the train you feel and hear your knees pop like gunshots.

"Mum," the child doesn't bother to speak softly or not to stare, "that lady's broke herself. I heard it."

"That's nice, darling," the mother returns, frowning at the Metro.

It's nearly a relief to know that those who can see you for what you are are mostly ignored by the rest of the world.

IV.

"Lemon sherbet with your paper, miss?" The man smiles as he sells you the paper. You check it every morning, sometimes you even grab an evening edition if you can spare the change, but nothing yet. Nothing so far. Once you would have said at least: "No, thanks though" but now you can barely manage to keep your swollen tongue in your mouth, forget flicking it round to make syllables out of air. You shake your head and look down, reasoning that there really isn't a reason to be polite, to carry on this façade of being human, alive, normal. But as you limp and creak your way home, thoughts swirl like diving birds and you think, Christ, if you don't keep going, observing the niceties despite all the decay, what's the point?

V.

You never thought you'd avoid being touched. You used to yearn for an embrace, friendly or romantic, it didn't matter. Just the press of skin on skin, the taut muscle sliding underneath. As you rot you dream of what it was like to feel warmth from another person. The weight of a mouth on yours. You see lovers and mothers and children and remember the first time you forgot and took the hand of a little girl who had fallen in the park, cut her knee. It was so long ago but you can still feel the scrape of your brittle skin over her smooth palm and the scuttle, the scream, the stare, the knowledge that you are a thing that shouldn't be and how maybe it was the first time you really knew it, too, how broken you were, how gone.

"What happened? Did that lady hurt you, darling?" The mother appeared then, her concern for her child, which had only a moment before been wrapped in a romance novel, seemed absolute.

You begin then to truly experience your existence teetering on the line between are and aren't and feeling the child's eyes on your back, you know that nothing is absolute. Especially love. You remember this each time you miss that last warmth.

VI.

It begins to feel like you're stuck in a Tube tunnel. Everything begins to echo, sounds elongate like they are made of taffy, stretching so far away from what you thought they were, assumed they could be, that you stumble about like a drunkard. Soon the world feels like it's wrapped in cotton batting and you can hardly make it down the block to the closest newsstand or Tube and you start to forget to care if you're being watched, you just want to know if anyone has missed you yet, reported you gone, wrote an obituary even. You'd settle for that, for their having given up on you, but nothing. Of course there's nothing. It's been forever and why would they start looking now?

You start turning chairs and dropping mugs and you wonder if the neighbors will care, complain, if they're banging the ceiling with a broom handle at this moment, but no, probably not, you don't feel anything, no vibrations, which you know you can still feel each night when the cat jumps onto your chest and purrs, your thinning ribs echoing empty.

VII.

You always cry when the last of your hair comes out. The first few times, you were so shocked, then so disgusted with yourself for believing that any part of you would survive that you tore the last chunks out yourself. You still hate yourself for caring so much about something so trivial, so stereotypically feminine. You try to remember what you thought about it when you were fully alive—were you a carefree and fuck all type or did you actually care if others thought you beautiful? You want to have been the former, though each time your hair becomes brittle enough to break off in your hands, threading into the crevices of your dry palms, you are at least somewhat certain that part of you cared very much. The balding ghost in the mirror stares at the metal glint of the clippers and promises to care less next time, to not cry, to rub the smooth scalp with oil like it's a thing that should be worshipped. You don't. Can't really. Any extras are too expensive and shopping for them might give you away.

VIII.

Your eyes begin to grey over. You've been in the apartment for what feels like forever, having stopped venturing out days ago. Weeks maybe. Time stops making sense without sound. It's a thing you couldn't ever have known when you were really living. When the film over your pupils thickens enough so that everything seems blanketed with mold, you barricade yourself in. You stack chairs and books and whatever was there when you first came and know that it won't be enough, it's never enough. Nothing can stop the dying, make sense of the process that finds you time and again.

Before you go completely blind you wash yourself—you always want to meet your maker clean—maybe like you were when he first found you, maybe not. You lie in the bath and cover yourself with water until you, you who is never cold, feel like you are made of ice. The water never stays in the tub (eventually all water returns to its source) and soon you find yourself naked and dry. You can barely see the lip of tub now, but you manage yourself out. You use your remaining vision, the remaining light, to slice open a bag of cat food, the bag you've been saving. Then you go to bed.

IX.

It seems unbelievable, but somewhere in the darkness of your chest, you can still feel your heart, a boxy vestigial organ. It stopped beating a long time ago. You can hardly even remember what it felt like. You imagine bombs detonating in your chest and all manner of hyperbole, but you know it was more like a constant knock below your collar-bone. You don't want to remember the next thing that snakes into your mind, of course you don't. You've wrapped yourself in sheets and quilts and overcoats; you've layered the hall with papers and furniture that presses the door and your feline protector stalks close by but still still still. Death's scent leaks into your mouth, pushes into your nose and up up up until it soaks your brain, your brain that is betraying you now now now how he tore through the layers of cloth and skin the night he couldn't quite take you, how he tears through them each and every time he finds you, yet leaves you to begin again, even now, even now, even now.

X.

You are asleep. Your brain has released your heart, your heart that was long dead and just didn't know it yet. Your limbs and teeth and lips are gone, your eyes and the delicate bones that curl like snails in the whorls of your ears, gone, all gone. This is the last thing that happens before it begins again. This time, there is a warm weight on your chest and it's vibrating deep inside you, it's stirring your organs back to life, it's nudging your chin and eyes with a rough tongue, it's asking you to wake up. Is this a dream, you wonder? Is it over? Is it just beginning? You have to open your eyes to find out.

APOCALYPSE PRACTICE

W hen did it start?" Monkey says with that mad gleam and of course, I don't have the heart to shut him up.

It was around All Hallows' Eve, I start, hoping he's done before I finish, parts of me hoping I am, too. The people upstairs were crazy for All Hallows', going on for weeks getting their gatherings and their fancy dress planned—

"What kind of fancy dress?" Monk wants to know, cough-spluttering already, and I want to tell him to save his breath, but damn I just can't. I just keep telling.

They liked dressing up and getting all sloshed one night a year, ghosts and goblins and all that, there were maps all over the bright tunnels to huge parties and places you could exchange paper cash for the creepiest threads. Back then, the bright tunnels were alive with upstairs people. Our people barely used the brights even then, of course, though some did. Some flitted between upstairs and down, carrying on in both. They were the ones who were there when the robes were discovered—

"They were never! Nan always said they only knew after the rats started—"

I tell him Nan was an old wife-teller, and he says the old ladies are the only ones left to tell the stories, only ones smart enough to survive.

He might be right. Not that I'll tell him.

Monk settles at last, and I start again.

In the tale I know, I say, challenging him to disagree with that, our boys had been keeping an eye on a dig that the upstairsers had been at for a few years, picking off all the broken tunnel tile and breaking in old walls from the Scollay for a bigger platform. We always kept an eye on upstairsers, enough to let them know that this territory was ours, even if they thought they owned it, and if they went too far, beyond where their lights stopped, we'd be there to turn them around.

The boys, their names are lost, but they knew what they saw when those workers busted that wall down, knew enough to get the hell out.

No one wants to be near the opening of a mouth to hell.

"But didn't any of the boys, maybe ... the bravest boy, think about warning the upstairsers?"

Well, I consider, maybe they hoped the workers'd be so rightly scared that they'd tell the upstairsers it was over: time to stop their dig, return the broken tile and dirt, and get out. Not that they'd be likely to believe anything a worker or one of us'd say. It's not that upstairsers are that dumb, it's that they ignore what's before them. They saw an old pile of rags and masks, just in time for their spooky parties, instead of what it was: all that was left of the last two sentinels that guarded the mouth.

Their bodies were long gone, locked inside that chamber more than a half-century before, all perished to dust but for the blood in the cloth, the bones that were sewn on bright as stars. That was death magic. And death magic, as long as it keeps where you put it, is dead powerful.

I stop for Monkey's laugh. He always laughs at that bit. Tonight, though, he is silent, so I go on.

Of course, now everything was broken. The new air crushed in and in moments ate away every spell, and the mouth was open and hell could pour out of it, and no one, not these upstairsers who laughed at the workers and who danced around under their glarish work lights with the blood-and-bone cloaks and the bone-splinter masks draped around them like at one of their All Hallows' parties, could stop it.

It was then the rats came, I emphasize, and I swear Monk harrumphs a bit then. They flooded the work site in minutes, chomping the upstairsers into pulp. The City (the upstairsers are in charge up there, sitting in their tall buildings, like they're gods without faces): they closed the site, said it was an unfortunate infestation brought on by the extreme chills of the past winters. At first, the upstairsers looked like they believed it. They kept using the brights, riding their metal cars all over underground.

Course we moved off, took to other tunnels. But odd things kept happening in the brights. Dead sharks appeared in the metal cars, flopping around on floors and dying in the air, only we didn't put them there. That in itself wouldn't be so bad, it could be unauthorized upstairser baiting (I remember the name for it from when we stole those pups, remember that?), but then the heads started to appear.

I pause, readying for the best part, the wickedest part, of the tale.

My dad, he saw them.

Monk doesn't interrupt. He knows not to scoff at anything I say about Dad.

It was so early that the moon was rushing in the tunnels that lead upstairs, coming straight down and bouncing off the tiles. There were some upstairsers on the platform but he thought he could sneak by and skulk into the shadows for a shortcut until this lady started screaming holy hell and there they were: about fifty heads all in a neat row. They're lined up on the do-not-cross line like they're anxious to get on the next car to come screeching down the tunnel. Heads would've been bad enough. Only these were demon heads. Many-eyed, flash-tongued, skinned and burnt. They were horrible.

It was then that we knew, he'd say, that we could move off, but it wouldn't stop what was coming through that hole, and we knew who'd get it first.

See, the sentinels had been put there to guard against the end times. To appease the darkness with a taste of blood, to know that we feared enough to sacrifice what was precious. And when they'd gone, hell figured it was time to move up, time to unleash and devour what was just below and then what was above.

It's getting dark in the hole now. So dark. And I hope I have time to finish the story. For Monk's sake. For my own.

Our people always knew the magic. Most didn't practice it much, but some did. It's why we could stay hidden downstairs, in the tunnels, beneath the rest. They had a big vote in the old stone hall in the under-center. So many thought that we could just stay put, that whatever would come would go straight for the upstairsers, the bloody chaos of above ground, leave our tunnels like the thin layer of under skin, too skinny to bite into. Others thought there was no escaping the ends that the mouth brought forth, that they'd seep into every crack and chomp up each little crump of living until nothing survived. There was no sure way to tell, and though we've always been more cautious than the people upstairs (we'd never have opened that vault in the first place, we know not to disturb the things that lie), we weren't prepared to admit that the end could come.

Even then, I whisper, shuffling closer to Monkey's clumpy body, we didn't want to see the evidence.

Of course, we know what happened then: some of us fled when the bloody teeth started filling our pockets and bags, and some of us woke with pulpy, empty mouths, and some didn't. More of us waited until the fingers of children got bitten off in the night, little stumps floating later in the drains like cigarette butts, and then finally, all the water turning to blood. We couldn't drink, we couldn't eat, we couldn't hold one another.

And so, a sacrifice was made. And at this I lean against the inside of the new bricks, the cement hard now under my touch, and breathe out for the first time in what feels like ages, for the last time maybe ever. Monk's face is still and the air is nearly gone and somewhere below me, I feel the earth churning, the ground opening up, ready to swallow us whole.

AND NOW WE LIVE ON A TRAIN UNDERGROUND

M iss Mags likes sitting near the doors, which is fine because she's old, or close enough to it. She once told me she likes to feel the whoosh of air when they slick open and slap shut.

"It reminds me of real air," she said, "country air." She was born somewhere upstate, in a tiny wooden spirit house, that's what she said, ghosts and demons and things knocking on her windows all times of night. I believed her at first, of course, because I was young when I started taking the train, wasn't I? I didn't know better then.

My mum was riding with me then—making sure that I didn't miss my stop, or linger later than I should—always worrying about someone snatching me up, like a wallet peeking from a back pocket or open purse. Like I'm that thick. I wouldn't go nowhere I didn't know I was sposed to go. I didn't have a death wish. Corey Starms got splatted that way. Slipped down a platform that was closed and an uptown train, I think it was the old K-line (not that it matters now), caught his beefy shoulder and there he went, all over the tracks.

Lines disappear sometimes—that's just what happens in cities old as ours. Stops get replaced, tunnels become weary of holding themselves up, and suddenly, there's no El. You have to M, Q, R down Atlantic Avenue if you want to make it to the other side of the river. Mum always said that the stops themselves sit and turn to dusty pockets underground and that if you look close you can see them as you're pushing through the quick dark on your way to where you're going. You can make them out real clear if you don't blink.

But where do the trains go, then, if they're from an old line? I'd ask. They can't just disappear, can they?

Mum would always answer quick, which is how I knew she didn't know, but didn't want me to worry.

"They send them for scrap, love. Use their parts to fortify our trains. Make sure they're the safest, the best."

I didn't know anything about ghost trains then, of course. Sometimes I wish I still didn't.

~

Mr. John is a jumper. He slides along the pearly blue benches and hums to himself. Other times he curls beneath them and cries to himself, his beardy face pressed into his muffler. Sometimes, when he's a bit manic (that's what Mum used to call it when I couldn't sit still), he swings the poles and sings. He says they're his poems and if everyone is in a good mood that day, we give him a clap. Other times, Mr. Hughes, who's normally the easiest bloke, even in the early mornings, says: "John, that's enough."

Once I thought I saw Mr. Hughes' dark face chuckle when Mr. John started spitting his poetry. Sometimes it's vulgar, not verse for the outside by any means, and Miss Mags starts shaking and hiccoughing and near vibrating herself into a fit, and Mr. Hughes has to take Mr. John to the back of the car and make him stay. Then Mr. Hughes comes back, face turned in, and opens his carry bag. Mr. Hughes writes verse, too, and it's like birds set off and flying in your chest when he reads it. Even Miss Mags says she loves it.

Most of the time, it's just the four of us, and somewhere, in the dark where we can't see, the engineers taking the train to its destination.

~

"Did you see them, child? The men in the masks?" Miss Mags is upset this morning. Her pink shawls and fringy skirts are all snaked around her and she's shaking like she really did see the ghosts she claims are everywhere.

What men? I say, thinking to myself that it's just one of her spirit dreams that she falls in to and out of on the long commute.

"The tunnel men ... their long faces ... there!" She points a stabby finger at the dirty windows and now I know it was a dream, it had to be. Them windows been covered-over with dust and grime for ages. Last time I saw through them, well, that was back when Mum was here, wasn't it?

It's ok, Miss Mags, I say, real polite like. No one's there.

Her face crumples at this and she just keeps repeating:

"They are. They are. They are there. They're there in the tunnel! Just look!"

I can see she's going to have a fit, and I don't like to bother Mr. Hughes, or get Mr. John started, not this early, not when there's so far to go, so I promise to sit next to her and watch for the tunnel men.

~

The tunnel men are another story, just like the old train stops. The tunnel men are workers with long masks on their faces who work day and night without rest in the deepest, darkest, oldest tunnels of the city. Their job is to seal over the old, unstable parts of the subway, which is creepy enough, but if you see them, you pretty much know your trip is done for because all they do is seal you in; they don't rescue you. When the trains started breaking down and the tunnels started caving, so many abandoned the trains. But my mum always said it was the fastest, safest, and best way to get where I was going. Even though she's not here and Miss Mags thinks the tunnel men are, I still think it's a better way than what some people do.

~

Mr. Hughes doesn't like my new job for Miss Mags. You can tell by the way his brow furrows and his moustache twitches.

"But the child has to be useful sometime, doesn't it?" Mr. John belches. He's what Miss Mags calls full of spirit today. "The child has to know sometime!"

The light in the back of the car flicks off for a few moments and then comes back on. Mr. Hughes is looking grim. Before I started taking the train, I heard some of the boys at my stop talking about how the lights failing is always a sure sign of a failing train, a train to retire soon. At the time, I didn't really listen. It was stupid Corey Starms anyway and it's clear how much of a stupid, know-nothing he was.

For a moment though, I do want my mum. The way she used to hold my hand when we first came here, to the city. It was always such an adventure. I bet it was dangerous, too. It's hard to keep together, especially now that the trains are so muddled. Better than back home, though, Mum would say.

~

I dream about the tunnel men. I don't mean to. I rarely sleep anymore, so it's a surprise when I open my eyes and realize I'm in it, a dream. I remember dreaming before I started taking the train, so I know what it feels like. Only this dream isn't like what I used to dream, not at all. In the dream the car is completely dark, the air heavy, like all the dust in the world is inside it. Somehow, I can see, which is a mystery but it's true. Everyone is in the car: Miss Mags, all twisted up in her pink skirts, Mr. John, for once not babbling or jumping about, just swathed in his thick muffler, and even Mr. Hughes, though his eyes are shut so tight they seem pushed into his brown face. I used to wonder if Mr. Hughes was my dad. It's a thought that seems silly now. Not that he couldn't be. Just that now it doesn't really matter, does it?

I hear bumps along the side of the car. The floor at my feet moves a bit, I think, though I can't feel it. To be honest, I can't feel a thing.

There's a skink sound of metal sliding on metal and the whole car jolts like it's alive again and it's going to take off now, fast, faster than fast, faster than the times Mum would swing me by my arms in the park, and for the first time I'm frightened. I don't want to go anywhere. Please, I say, don't make me go.

There's the slap of the doors opening for the first time in ages and not even Miss Mags moves to catch a breath of air, and these horrible grey snouts press into the space where the doors were just seconds ago and I say, please, please, please, let me stay. Over and over and over.

But of course, I'm not really saying anything, am I? None of us can say anything now.

∾

"You fell asleep, dear." Miss Mags smooths her fingerless gloves over her skirt.

I did, I say.

The air in the car feels crisp today. Like autumn. What I remember of it.

"Do you feel better?"

I look about at Mr. Hughes, reading papers from his satchel. Perhaps Mr. John will have a good day and they'll both read to us on our way. I try and remember if this has ever happened before. Not that it matters now. The air around me feels light and I know that the tunnel men are just a dream, that we're on our way, and we'll get there. Yes. The tunnel men will never find us.

THE NEW HEROES AT THE OLD FAIRGROUNDS

The drive-in is as grey as a grave—the shroud of the screen flanked by fly-away ribs from the old fairground rollercoaster. Old beaters like ours fill the lot: a lawn of dull tin spread before the bombed-out building where our home used to be, before the blaze that got the roller-coaster devoured everything.

Grey hunks of cement rise, wall me in flashing memories of old publicity posters (all elongated spines and sharpened teeth). Now it's just us, two-thirds of a family of forgotten freaks, hunch-backed in the rusty pickup. You watch creature features; I try to tell stories of your childhood, the flames that consumed it.

You lie, say your dream-memories are filled with sticky teacup seats and carousel unicorns. The memory of your mother's laugh floods me, muddying the mats on the floor of the pickup truck, while fake monsters and madmen mutate into bigger, better versions of us. Are we no longer feared?

Our new heroes fill the gull-pecked screen of the drive-in, negate our blood and shroud our bonehome—the space where the Bearded Lady and JoJo the Dog-faced Boy barked, where your small life began, where your mother's ended.

The roar of the Wolfman mimics the bellow of the fire that danced in our apartment. In my dreams, it dulls to a midnight blue buzz behind my ears, but here it hums loud.

Here at the drive-in, it explodes: floods me with those slicked faces, large men grown larger with drink, throwing Molotov cocktails through our kitchen window.

Your mother's laughing scream fills the gravelly spaces in memories you keep saying you are too young to remember clearly, memories I need you to carry, memories I try to rescue from the floor of the pickup each time you drop them, will yourself to forget.

The only thing you say you remember is this: your grandmother's efficiency apartment at the Capri Motel, where songs from the 50s filled the steamy bathroom and she taught you to read fortunes from smoke, predict dreams but for a price.

She told you: every where and when but here and now is but an afterthought, my starlet, a ghost whisper as real as the triumphs and screams of final girls and damsels in distress on screen.

And you listened. You remembered.

Not to the filling cry of your mother that floods me like a wolf roar, not to the backdraft bawl of your nightmares, not to the voice, the laugh, the scarlet scream of your mother in the memory you refuse to hear.

THE CHILDREN'S HOUSE

We never find the house, not the way other children would. Never follow a hardball through a bramble lot so we can continue some childhood game. We dream it, all of us at once, the ether of night and star perfuming our imaginations until we conjure what we need and it falls from the sky of our minds, appearing in front of us, milky windows and solid shingle.

Inside are all the children we have ever been. The ephemera of who we were is carefully catalogued: jars full of baby teeth line the pantry shelves, dresses and trousers clotted with dirt, blood, spit (and other excretions that we don't understand yet) stand in tiny closets, button fronts pressing to zipper backs. Sometimes we slide between the limp shirts and sweaty robes and breathe deep, all the particles of the children we used to be settling, for a moment, inside our mouths.

No one suspects us, not at first. Our parents serve us lunches of white bread and mustard and meat, sugary pink drinks and cakes before sending us on to summer adventures. They hardly ever miss the torn things, worn things, the things that we spirit away. But sometimes, we are caught out: the clink of a broken tumbler in a paper bag, the clang of silver in our pockets (we have a ceramic bank in the shape of an animal on the mantle where we store coin—we took it long ago, back when we still desired families with other children). When the eyes of our parents start to narrow, we know it is time to move on.

It is never difficult to leave our parents. We have done it so many times before. Each in our separate beds, we conjure dreams again. Only this time, each dream is a bit different: one set of parents lights matches over kerosene heaters, another tucks thick towels in the cracks around the kitchen door, lock themselves in, turn on the gas. In others, there are guns. These streams of dream stuff never fail to ignite action, frantic and self-obsessed. And our parents forget about us. We leave freely. There is no reason to tip-toe on creaking clapboard anymore and we slip out of our old houses, our old selves, and make our way to new ones.

Our house always reappears with us. Our parents, our real parents, many galaxies away, will one day collect the evidence that we have gathered. And on the nights after the conjuring of our house but before the leaving, we wonder, dreaming of stars, stars that were once our real homes, but are now just memory and dream-dust, if our real parents yearn for our return.

HANSEL AND GRETEL

After she killed the old lady, my sister became obsessed with ghosts. Searching the grey midwestern landscape for weeks, we finally found the most haunted place we could imagine. Rosebud State Asylum looked like it had grown up out of the forest of some maniac's imagination. Its crumbling brick face was overgrown with the kind of florescent greenery that threatened to spread and choke the barren yellow fields surrounding it. Wet roots twined over the bottom edges of windowsills like huge eyelashes, and the loose floor tiles slid over the threshold like a broken tongue. The whole place should have tumbled to dust years ago; something stronger than swollen oak and rusting steel must have been holding it together.

Once we passed through those doors, I felt trapped, as if we were sealed inside a tiny box full of hot breath. I wanted to run back out into the cool emptiness of the dead fields, back to the rotting orphanage, back; at least there, I knew what to fear. But my sister wouldn't go back. Her entrance was irrevocable, like the part of her soul that had burned up in the fire pit along with the old lady's dry bones. And for kids like us, the best way is never to go back to the beginning.

The best way is to forget what you did, who you were. For some people, it's hard. Gretel says there must be hundreds of ghosts stuck here, bodiless murderers and pedophiles and lunatics who can't forget what they did. She says she can see their hollow faces, can feel their rotten teeth scrape her ears. She says the ghosts tell her what to do, how to go on now that she's done something most people only dream of doing, something that most people, once they've done it, want to take back. She doesn't say anything about how I should go on, though I can hear her drop my name into the middle of the barren, rancid rooms, like a stone into a shallow pond, a question into the stale air. She says they don't answer when she asks about me. But I think she's lying.

No matter what story you've heard, she was always the clever one. The one with the last chicken bone, the pebbles smoother than pearls. I was the one with the impractical stomach, the taste for breadcrumbs and gingerbread. She's always been my saving grace, telling me when to stay put and when to run.

Last night, she folded herself into a cramped, polyester-lined casket in the mortuary viewing room, her dirty arms crossed over her chest. I think she was pretending she was already a ghost. "Tomorrow," she whispered, "we'll look for the boiler room and get warm for good. They'll never find us."

I didn't want to go to the boiler room; the razor-cut air already clawed, wrapped itself around my throat, making it difficult to breathe.

Gretel didn't seem to notice; her face smoothed into blankness as soon as she closed her eyes. I sat in a corner of the room, sweated, and waited for sleep to come. I found papers moldering in a gunmetal cabinet and read about the people who used to live here, the things they did to be called insane. Gretel always says people don't have to be insane to do insane things. She says everyone's capable of madness, of death. It's just that some people get caught.

~

My sister is curled beside me, cool hands smoothing my hair behind my ears and rubbing my temples. Suddenly her breath is a muggy ghost on my cheek, her hand a poker, jabbing me into a mountain of steamy ash. I open my eyes and my gasp is lost in the yawning cavity where her face used to be. "Follow me, Hansel," the non-face of my sister says. And just when I feel her fingers curl around my throat, she disappears. And I'm alone, tucked into a sharp corner of this damp room for the dead, trying to catch my breath somewhere in the sticky air. It's barely dawn, the tiny pebbles of starlight shifting through the half-torn blinds.

I stumble to the viewing casket, jerking and frantic through the cloying smell of formaldehyde floating in the air. It is empty, yet the polyester bed is blistered, as if the body within had suddenly burst and scorched it to become ash, now dusting the floor in feet-shaped cakes. I follow the ashy footsteps into a hallway, puce paint peeling away from the red muscle of the walls, windows gnashing glass teeth. The window yawns wide, opening onto a brick courtyard where carelessly tossed bones simmer in a cement pool half-filled with putrid green water. On the lip of the window I find a stone, almost perfectly round and black as onyx. I roll it in my fingers. It's warm from the hand that dropped it here, not long ago.

I see another black stone, glinting at me like an eye in the far corner of the hall. I don't want to go further into this house of ghosts. I don't want to be swallowed by their hollow faces, drowned in an inferno of hot breath.

I've followed Gretel all my life, through scab-kneed jeans, behind dumpsters hiding from whatever monsters the orphanage decided we belonged to that month, into the death of that old witch that stole us away, and here, where black teeth bite and empty faces swallow until there is nothing left.

I stand in the hall, bleeding walls and shattered glass closing in, and even though I've always followed, I feel a pulling at the base of my skull, telling me that the way out is through the fields, into the woods, not through these decaying rooms, not inside the hot belly of this place, the warmth of the boiler.

And before I can decide, I hear my sister's voice telling me to follow. And I run.

POSTCARDS FROM THE UNDERWORLD

I. Mother Love

To: Persephone, The World, General Delivery

~~From~~ Love: Your Mother

Where are you?

Can't you tell me? Even me?

Zeus keeps bringing me roses. He says he can't make you come back, that Eurydice is a loose cannon he should have dealt with long ago. He doesn't say he's sorry. I let him drip rain on the front porch and let the roses die.

The cat keeps pining for you. I forget to feed her sometimes and then she reminds me with a sharp bite. When did I get so forgetful?

I miss your long hair, the snarls I brushed out when your arms were too tired. If you come home, I won't forget you.

Love,

Mom

To: Demeter

From: Persephone

Mom,

Just stop it. That cat is old and deaf and can barely tell you're there. She never cared for anyone but Zeus. And you know what? He liked her more than us. He never wanted a family, just a pet.

P

PS—I haven't had long hair since I was seven. Remember? I fell asleep chewing that minty gum one of your nympho friends left behind and it got stuck in my hair like a sticky green web. We had to get that old lady next door, the one who had sharp scissors from the weaving factory, to cut it out. I cried. You said that's what I get for being careless. Carelessness loses love, you said. Then a few nights later Zeus split, leaving his old cat and his record collection. "He said I wasn't beautiful anymore, that I no longer made myself beautiful just for him," you said.

When I reminded you about carelessness making losing what you love your own fault, you slapped me. I didn't miss Zeus. I still don't.

II. The Lovers, or Eurydice and Persephone in Tornado Alley

We sit under the dark bruise of Oklahoma sky, her hands in my lap. It didn't start like this: braiding hair and coy mouths peeking from behind clammy palms. It was all hot mouth on my neck, thumbs pressing elbows. Tumbleweeds crowd the car and dust swirls the heavens green, and instead of being soft our bodies are hard—too heavy to be torn away from the earth.

Neither of us thought of going to hell; of becoming concubine or shade.

III. Breaking Out

She leaned in close, blood from her lips staining the skin just below Persephone's ear and whispered: "This is how you kill a god."

$\sim$

The shades taught her how to take it all away with just one kiss. Eurydice's black hair tangles in his hands as she pushes him against the alley wall. His bare arms are bar-floor sticky, slick with sweat and he sighs into her open mouth. He tastes eager and young, mouthwash over cheap beer. She sucks his breath, his memory away. As he loses himself to her, she slides her hand around his sweaty back, unhooks the keys on his belt. She wants to keep going, make it all the way out of here, snuff him out like a candle for being so stupid as to fall for a mysterious woman in a grungy bar. His gasps for air make it difficult to stop but this is more than a tryst, it's her get-out-of-jail-free card, so she squeezes his shoulder and steps back as he drips to the ground like dirty rainwater. In a few moments he'll blink bleary eyes at the sky, know the names and locations of all the stars and great constellations but not who he is.

"Cassiopeia?" He calls after her.

But she's already backing out of the alley, toward the dark blue Chevy Impala she spied him driving earlier tonight. She wants to be well away from the Underworld when the Queen kills her King. Eurydice hadn't been sure that Persephone would help her, but the Queen's memory was long, a grey snake that squeezed her heart until it was ash. She was only half-god, a trophy still that Hades displayed for the denizens of the Underworld as proof of his power over the living and the dead. The shades and harpy-ghosts would riot of course. Would kill the Queen, surely. Or at least try. Eurydice pushes the Impala into the last gear, feels the hooves of a thousand horses beneath her and hopes it's enough.

She's got a long way to go before the sun rises.

ASPHODEL

The Waters of Forgetfulness don't always work the way they're supposed to. Lots of people remember everything. Some say there's more than one kind of water—that the Waters of Memory are also on tap. I wouldn't know, myself.

from *The Penelopiad* by Margaret Atwood

When she wakes up in the afterlife, wrapped in yards and yards of white sheets, Penelope thinks it's a cruel joke. Is she meant to lie still in a cotton cocoon for all eternity? Be as bound to woven string as she was in life? Yet she unwinds, crawls out of the web of thread, and finds herself in a room full of colorless cloth—polyester, pleather, clean banks of cotton that seem to float through ceiling and floor, the whiteness running on forever. Her shroud sticks to her ankles and wrists. She makes her way to the cutting table and grabbing a pair of bone-handled scissors, cuts the fabric away. She feels light now and starts to notice others, wriggling in their fabric sacks, lazily slithering out. She tries counting how long it takes for them to unweave themselves but without breath, she's not sure what a minute is anymore. She can't even be certain of a second. Without life, time doesn't exist.

This is what the afterlife is: a department store filled with the absence of things, their facsimiles lining all the shelves—racks and racks of colorless costumes in the clothing department, nuns' wimples and nurses' caps, uniforms that distinguish nothing, poking and curling through a fabric sea; knives and cauldrons bleached clean; crystal display cases full of bottles and tubes of milky perfumes that smell faintly of memory and then fade to nothing. The dead roam the floors of the afterlife like a Woolworth's—floating toward whatever object is closest, fingering the hems and blades and glass edges. Some she knows, remembers: cousins, maids (the young ones her son had hanged for betraying their house looked as if they'd never seen her before; she had expected them to run from her, to beg forgiveness, to tear her dead flesh). Everyone wraps themselves in their costumes and carries baskets of flowers and do not seem to know her, or anything at all.

White is the color of death, the absence of things and in the afterlife, it seems, all are encouraged to be absent. The only things that live are the asphodel trees: their blooms burst from walls and hang over beds and booths in the restaurant where the dead eat the flowers directly from the overhanging branches and sip the dew that runs down the boughs and trunks and into the fountains that spring up by every seat, every shelf, every display.

Penelope watches and waits. She's always been very good at waiting. At patience. She weaves loose threads from her tunic through her fingers and sees her cousin, Helen, who many say started it all, and waves. Helen glides over, angelic light pooling around her head and neck.

"Hello, Cousin!" Helen, giddy in death as in life, sits beside Penelope.

"Hello."

"Have you tried the asphodels today? They taste simply marvelous!

And that scent from the perfume counter—let me give you a splash ..."
Helen rummages in her cracking woven basket.

Penelope doesn't know exactly how to handle Helen. She never did.
Penelope was always the placid one, the one who thought and remembered and brooded, but she can't believe that Helen would greet her as if nothing had happened.

"Have you seen my father?" Penelope manages.

Helen looks blankly at her. A full bloom hangs from her pasty lips, partially devoured. She points to a young man in a crisp linen suit and fedora walking by.

"Perhaps, that is him?"

Penelope believes it must be an act, a cruel act to manipulate her, to get a reaction, until petals slick with spit fly out of Helen's mouth and she greets Penelope again, as if she has only just seen her.

"Hello, cousin! Try the asphodels today; they're to die for!" Helen's smile is insipid, her pupils dilated.

The scent of the crushed asphodels burns her nose and she finds that, for a moment, she wants to let go of the Helen she knew, to simply forget her.

∼

Penelope remembers everything. She always has. It's a relief that death hasn't changed that. She is frightened after her meeting with Helen. Frightened that she will lose herself, become not a ghost but an absence. It's something she feels she can't bear: if she doesn't have herself, she has nothing.

Penelope avoids Helen, avoids those rancid blooms and their sticky sap. She stalks the aisles of kitchen and housewares, reimagining and re-remembering her life. She starts with the cutlery, runs her thumb along the sharp blades of fish knives and recalls her first memory. It's as well-worn as her fingers were after that score of weaving years, and each time she re-remembers the truth, she recreates, slightly alters, adds, subtracts, conflates. Her mind does all kinds of mathematical feats until the memory is remade into the thick cotton batting of story, while the truth remains a cloud wisp whose shape remains elusive.

This is what she remembers: swirling and spiraling, the cold waves of the Adriatic close over her. She is a tiny, flesh-colored stone sinking to the bottom of the darkened cove below her childhood home. Each detail of the story becomes a jewel, precious and faceted. She holds fast to the waters of this memory, in fact, she welcomes the waves that splashed at the stones beneath her nursery window, the belief that they could never, ever harm her. Hadn't they greeted her every morning? A million shades of blue sky and green land and grey eye of her father? It is all about him, after all; he is the center. And as the sea once again swallows her whole, she marvels at how she did not wonder where her father was, why he wasn't saving her (of course, this is really all she wonders, has wondered, for the whole of her life), why she looked only into the murky depths as if they held her answers. She does not remember that she threw her own son into the sea when he was days old, sad and heavy from recent birth and her husband far away, testing the tale she'd heard that all babies can swim, can regrow their fins and tail and float away on muscle memory.

Instead, Penelope lives completely, again and again, in what happens next, the actions that help her shape her father's soul.

The water turned grey as it deepened, like her father's eyes, and she welcomed it, sought it, until a large hand pressed her small skull into this womb, drowning her. Far beneath the salty umbilical fluid, she heard a voice:

"Leave her to the sea gods to scavenge, then." The voice was cold, a jagged rock, and the grey water began to rush into white sky then, biting her tiny feet and hands, and then she floated in another sea, one made of sand and air and almost breath. She woke staring into her father's cold eye, his hand wrapped beneath her chin, his elbow crushing her breast bone. She does not move. Does not take her eye from his eye, the grey umbilicus, the cold pupil. Even when the oracle pulls him away stating, with murky words she has to strain to hear, that the sea god must have had a reason for rejecting the sacrifice.

Penelope never wants to forget this. She: a perfect oval, a brown egg that fell and floated and despite it, survived.

∽

Silence makes him nervous, she thinks, as he leans out of his seat, white vinyl booth squeaking as he dips his glass into the cloudy fountain.

"So ... come here often?" Icarius's manner is easy, and Penelope remembers suddenly how charming he was when she was young. How he'd sweep her mother into his arms and dance her around the dinner table. She hasn't thought of him in that way in years, tries to push the memory away, submerge it in cold waves and drown it, but it's so vivid: the red of her mother's shift, the careful border that Penelope had embroidered herself: golden naiads dancing in the sun. The sound of her father laughing and the quick, keen movements of his hands, his feet, as he swirled her mother in and out of chairs, the floating green fronds of palms sticking to their cheeks as they passed.

Icarius smiles at Penelope's silence and offers her a milky glass full of dew. She shakes her head and he winks at her, slips a penknife from an inside pocket of his robe and runs the dull blade along one of the small branches that hang low over the table at which they sit.

"How about this, then?" He offers her the cluster of asphodel, tight-lipped buds pressed shut, the promise of sweetness held inside. "The best in the place!"

He laughs and in spite of herself, Penelope hears the echo in her mind, the hallways of thought light instead of dark, tumbling with poppy-colored, gold-rimmed cloth instead of freezing, icy sea air.

"I'm not hungry," Penelope says. She imagined that she'd be venomous, sharp, cutting like her scissors and instead she is dull, unsure, homesick almost, for a man who has haunted the waters of her memory, who does not resemble the man before her.

Penelope's fingers itch for her needles, for the scissors that have occupied her as she remembered and re-remembered, her life, her death. Anything to occupy her hands, to still the creep in her stomach. Icarius's smile softens and he asks if she is in a hurry to leave.

Where would I go if I were? she thinks.

He has finished his plate of buds and is wresting another serving from the overhanging tree, his hands tangled in the branches.

"Did you know I was married?" His voice surprises her, wafts into her ears from the mouths of opening buds. She looks into the branches: creamy flowers obscure his face. His eyes are as milky as the asphodel.

"Yes," he continues, "I was quite important when I was alive. A king!

With gold and wives and scores of children." He recites his story as if it is a fairy tale. "My first bride was a princess, a naiad. Why, you can imagine how her father, the king of the gods himself, reacted when he found out she was thick with my child. Me, a mere mortal! They're all dead now, of course. All of them. Though I've never seen them."

The man across from her is no longer looking at her, no longer listening, has possibly forgotten that she is there. White buds stick in his beard and she thinks if she were a better daughter she would pick them out for him. She pulls instead on her own thick braid and counts to ten. Waits for her hands to stop shaking.

Icarius sits, wipes the sweat from his emptying glass and frowns as he speaks, as if he remembers something. He takes a sip from the cool glass and his faces relaxes. Penelope sees this happen a thousand times a day, an hour, a minute; whatever time is here, however it is or is not measured, it is full of forgetting.

"So what did you want to talk about?"

How did I ever think this was going to work? She thinks of the endless sharpening of scissor blades, the re-remembering of the moment that made her who she is, made her choices for her for the rest of her life.

"Why did you sacrifice your daughter?" Her voice is high and sharp and neither of them recognize it.

"Are you my daughter?" Icarius's eye widen, though it isn't clear to Penelope that he knows the meaning of the word daughter, how it differs from wife, servant, even king. His words are without malice, curiosity, or even concern. He strokes his beard and white buds fall over his lap, a snow of memories he can't quite catch on his tongue.

"You tried ... you sacrificed her to the sea god like an animal." She spits at him. She's practiced this part over and over, yet she can never say it the way she needs to say it, can never get all the details to behave the way she wants them to. This is the key, she thinks, to why she's been surrounded by men who tried to drown her and still expected her to love them: her husband who left for 20 years to chase fame and myths and whores, her son, the suitors, but first her father, her father who tried to drown her, once in the sea, once on land. Maybe if she can understand this, she can understand how everything in her life went so horribly wrong.

The asphodel continues to fall like snow from his beard. Soon it is all around them, a cloud of petals sliding over the table, sticking to her fingers and lips, getting caught on her tongue. She tries and fails to spit them all out.

"Cloudburst, table 4!" trumpets from an unseen loudspeaker. Soon, she knows, this will all be swept away, forgotten.

"I had scores of children," Icarius repeats, "and a beautiful half-god wife, and gold to make Midas blush!"

He sits and opens his hands wide; asphodel buds gather like dew drops on the lines etched heavily into his palms. Before she can stop herself, Penelope reaches across the table and snatches his hands, crushing his words and the flowers, grinding them between their palms.

"No, Icarius. You had but one child. A princess." Her words raze her throat, his throat, with their truth. Why do we always forget the woman, the girl? Why are they blank but for the sweet of their sex or quick cunning?

Icarius's thick brows shake, shiny as sea-snakes and he pauses as if he is about to remember, about to say something real, to verify the stormy colors of the sea and Penelope's cold breath on his hands.

"There was a boy once, a prince perhaps, a serving boy. He could swim like a duck. Pápia, we called him. I often wondered if my naiad bride had taught him her watery ways. Yet the seas took him. Of all the sons that I fathered or perhaps didn't, he was my favorite. A golden egg, a brilliant boy. The oracles said his death was destined." The old king's voice softened and the asphodel piled around them in sheets, blanketing them, snaking about their arms and covering them so completely that no one could see that they still clasped hands, ground the asphodel between sticky palms; no, their crushing grip could never have been seen, only touched softly under layers and layers of snow-white buds.

"It was a girl," Penelope whispers. And she tells him the story again. The story she has told herself for so long. This time, the story feels far away, a balloon filled with flowers, floating farther and farther from her body. The story is now neither who she is or who she was. She is tired. And this time it is just a story.

Icarius is no longer listening. His cup is full of flowers and Penelope rises, brushes the asphodel from his shoulders, empties his cup, dips it slowly into the fountain that flows past them, the stream that never stops. She places the cup between them and runs her finger along the wet lip, presses the sweet forgetfulness over her gums.

SEARCHING

1962

Matty stands in front of the bathroom mirror. The steam from the tap billows up and clouds the glass and in the clouds he tries to see his father. The metal of the razor slides up his throat, scrapes away the thick stubble that shrouds his features. He started shaving last year, at eleven, and now he does it every day, scraping the black hair that takes over by the time afternoon rolls around. His mother can't stand to look at him now; even though his skin in winter still stays nearly as Irish pale as hers, and his hair as black, he is clearly this other thing: skin that darkens to tree bark, body covered in a soft carpet of thick, curled mane. Recently, he found his birth certificate. Hidden away with pictures that disappear and are never seen again, he learned that he's a Mateo not a Matty, or a Matthew, not the clearly white bread American his Irish immigrant mother so wants for her children. His father, who he doesn't remember, was Brazilian, born in Recife, a cutter at the factory that still tells the hours from its tower clock in the city where he and his mother and three siblings sleep. He's a carbon copy, his older sister says. That's why ma was so hard. He was exactly what his father was.

∾

1991

The whirl of grasshoppers and trill of birds calms his blood. He can feel the forest cool his skin through the hoodie as he climbs the hill then descends into the Fort Lee woods. He knows every tree root and stone wall, but he waits until he gets further in. He keeps his eyes to the path, hoping to see at least a black racer or even a tiny garter snake on his way to the falls. This part of the fort is well-traveled: beer cans fill hollowed-out tree stumps and paths are well-worn.

Still, he examines the bark of the trees carefully, noting mostly new engravings: CM and KP, Tony loves Shelley forever 1989, Tony loves Sara forever 1990. He even catches himself searching for the tiny initials he carved into the trunk years ago when his daughter was small. He let her hold the jackknife and make the first mark. It wasn't deep enough to stay; the tree gave up that bark coat long ago. He hasn't seen what he hopes to see: the long, deep scratches that tell him that he's close. That he'll see the beast soon, someday, ever. It doesn't stop him from looking. Making his way into the deep woods, far from the rustic benches and fire pits of teens, back to where Matty's been searching for bigfoot for nearly all his life.

∾

1964

"Are you serious?" His younger brother, Peter, exclaims. "You're just being ridiculous. Ask ma."

His brother goes back to organizing his boxes of pencils into neat, perfect rows in a small shoebox. Presentation is everything, he tells Matty. The next day in school, Pete will sell pencils to his classmates for a dime each, and will make a killing until one of the nuns catches him and calls his mother, who will sweep down into the school, her tongue sharp as her widow's peak, and pull him away by his ears.

Matty won't ask ma anything. He is the one who sits up with her in the dark when everyone else is asleep (sleep will elude him, as it did her, for his entire life) and watch monster movies. Even after she married their stepfather, who sleeps like the dead, comes with a pioneer name, and has little time left for his stepchildren after disciplining them, they sit up together, the constant smoke of her Newports glaring off the television, rubbing against Dracula's creamy cheeks. Because of all this, he knows monsters are real and he is not afraid, because they are out there. He's going to find one, hunt it down, prove it.

No matter where the stepfather moves them, he'll sneak out at night and find the woods, the swamp, he'll walk until the light starts blinking from the sky.

~

2016

Dad called today. From a cabin, a ranger station, somewhere in the Wyoming woods. He's making his way inland after spending so much time north and west for so many years.

"Visibility is low," he says. The western mists are strangling the sight of the team.

He's been gone for so long, you wonder when he'll run out of forest. When he covers North America, will he jump the Panama Canal? Paddle through rice-fields, searching the green-bladed landscape for watery footprints?

You don't remember when he wasn't doing this. Even before he left your mom, your stepmom, he spent hours in the woods, first the northeastern forests he grew up in, and then the southern swamps. He glimpsed all sorts of creatures, your weekly phone calls full of water moccasins, corn snakes, even wild boar, and the occasional wispy rumor of Florida panther. Shadows bloomed like toadstools in the rain of your conversations. He'd always been obsessed.

Then the call. That's what it is in your mind: the call. His first real proof (according to him, he'd known for years, though this, this was the undeniable truth that would make everyone believe him). He'd called you right away, before he phoned his wife at work at the Piggly Wiggly. It made sense to you; she'd become less tolerant of his strange hobby over the years, and to be honest, you can't blame her, she had to live with him.

You were fourteen, on your way to some goth show in some basement where the walls were painted red like blood and the boys were older. Whatever you were doing in those days. You can't always recall.

"They're definitely out there." He huffed into the phone, like he'd been running.

"What, Dad? Hunters?" You'd always been a worrier. You'd think about him so far away, walking the swampy woods, especially in the fall when hunters were known to shoot anything that moved, even if it was in your own front yard, animal or human. You had nightmares where his small frame limped along the country lane where he lived, arrow sticking out of his leg, bleeding a red ribbon down the road.

"Sasquatch. I finally heard one."

"What?"

"I was doing my walk in the woods, and at about the third rest stop I crushed my last can, and I just couldn't resist, I thought, what the hell? I'll try it."

"Try what?" You were smudging black lipstick on your eyelids, puffing powder on your cheeks and neck, trying to look whiter, getting more bored than worried.

"I tapped it." He paused. You didn't respond so he went on: "The beer can. Three times, tap, tap, tap, on the tree trunk. And someone, something," he paused, corrected himself, "knocked back! I heard the echo through the woods, clear as day. So I knocked again."

You pictured your father crouched by a tree, several beers in, empty cans rattling in his backpack, throwing smooshed cans at the winter-peeled bark. It was ridiculous. And sort of scary. Weird. All of those things.

"Maybe it was a woodpecker?" You hated that he was like this. You put more lipstick on.

"It was Bigfoot, I'm telling you. Normal people and animals don't knock back like that."

You're right, you thought. Normal people don't.

You didn't say that though. You don't remember what your exact response was. You were young. Craving escape from your life of gloomy music and detention and depressing books.

What you said never mattered anyway. He ended the call like he always did: told you to call your grandmother soon and hung up.

~

1965

Matty sits in front of the television; his stepfather isn't home so he and his brother get to choose channels. Tonight is a National Geographic special called "The Legend of the Yeti." Their stepfather won't be home for hours. He's out playing cards and will come home drunk. Drunker than usual. Ma is in the kitchen with Aunt Kate, brandied hiccoughs and cigarette smoke punctuating their growled conversation.

"The yeti, as he is known in the Himalayas, is one of earth's most mysterious and elusive creatures. But is he real at all? Sherpas and mountaineers, even park rangers in the United States of America have claimed to see the man-beast."

The television is bright. Matty stares at the concave screen, the thick forests and night beyond, the castings of footprints that are familiar, even to him, but that many experts say are no real proof. He sees each piece of evidence as concrete, a thing to be touched and therefore tangible evidence of an existence everyone wants to deny but can't.

"That is incredible." The black of the forest flicks to a commercial for dish soap.

"What a load of rubbish," Pete says. "What a fake." Pete's not even looking at the TV. He's sharpening Ticonderogas, half-sawing off the erasers of otherwise perfectly good pencils with a razor so his class-mates will have to buy more.

"How can you say that? People all over the world have seen him, Pete! This thing is real!"

"Yeah, sure." Pete doesn't care about anything except what's right in from of him.

"Dumbass." Matty says, starting a fight that will result in a broken pencil and being grounded and a beating from his stepfather, who says he doesn't enjoy disciplining them but surely, surely does.

~

1966

Matty is home sick. It's Saturday and he is sixteen and not even his stepfather could make him go out with the family, who are visiting Auntie Della. He's too old for that, he thinks, curling deeper into the scratchy wool blanket and trying to focus on the monster movie in front of him. Giant rabbits with tusk-like fangs are destroying the planet and an Alan Alda look-alike is trying to save the day.

He's not sure how many times the phone rings; his head is hot and his mouth is dry and it seems to take him forever to stumble to the phone.

"This is a collect call from Saint Mary's, California. Will you accept the charges?"

Matty doesn't know anyone from California, nor where Saint Mary's even is, but on the programs he watches and books he reads as often as he can, the experts say bigfoot is known to be seen in the

Sierra Nevadas, and he thinks that's in California so he says yes, yes, he'll accept them.

The voice on the other end slurs and says: "Hannah?"

He knows and doesn't know that the name belongs to his mother, who has only gone by Ann for as long and as far as he knows. Who would have known his mother as Hannah? Not even her sisters call her that. They all adopted American names, dropping their "haytches," and calling the press the dresser or the closet. Preferring coffee to tea.

"No …" Matty wonders what he should say. Is this him? The man he's known existed for so long? His cheeks feel like they are full of bees.

The line clicks. Goes dead. Matty holds the plastic phone until it slips from his sweaty palm. Later, his stepfather will yell about who left the phone off the hook and his mother, for once, will say nothing. Replace the phone in its plastic receiver and stare.

~

Today

You never know these things about your father, at least not until it's too late for understanding to do either of you any good. You have accepted that he shadows the dark man living in the woods, the missing link, the proof that we're all just animals anyway. This is something that he has to do. And you, your job has been to listen. To catalog and say, yes. Someday you'll reach the road with the dark shape at the end of it and you'll be done. And then you will either lay down right there or you will turn around. Either way you will come home.

AFTERIMAGE

It's only temporary, she'd told herself, gripping the vinyl gloves, their empty plastic fingers braided with hers. The sign at student affairs had said that it was good money and it was: enough for film, darkroom supplies, maybe books for next semester, meager bowls of hot pot ramen and instant cream of wheat.

The first week had been busy: a four-body week, Mel had said, though not in front of the sons, granddaughters, partners that were left behind, browned pine and Douglas fir needles sticking to their shoes, tiny bones of Christmas trees punctuating loss. It was important that they did not speak to the grieving. The left-behind were not supposed to be there, not when the cleaners did their work.

Each time Sam walks through the kitchen doors, the side entry, the back, she is astounded by the pictures in front of her, the tension between the emptiness and the small impressions that the now-dead left behind, fingerprints in trails of sugar, reading glasses tucked into last week's newspapers, the light on the curtains, sometimes freshly pressed and sometimes draped with cobwebs, mugs and half-filled coffee cups abandoned on counters.

"You're on food today," Marina had told Sam that morning when she picked her up at her dorm. Marina speaks Spanish to her when they are alone, and English when they are with the rest of the clean-up team. Four can efficiently break down a family-sized home in a day. The team is Marina, Mel, and Don, a retired Vietnam vet—or so he claims—and finally, when Don and Mel refused to touch the kitchen because of the horrible smells, the sadness of a half-eaten banana, Marina had hired Sam.

Are you a hard-worker? Do you enjoy working with your hands? Call Marina at 900-CLEAN-UP! Good pay and flexible hours. At first, Sam had thought it must be some kind of sexy maid thing, which she didn't think she'd be willing to do, for whatever money.

"Sí?" Marina's voice had been sharp, impatient on the phone line. Sam hesitated, as she did these days—answer in Spanish or in English? Be familiar or a stranger? Sometimes it worked in her favor—the cafeteria staff passed extra scrambled eggs and extra strong cups of coffee over the counter, sometimes waved her change away at the register, giving instead: "Hasta pronto! Classe, no?"

The receiver cupping her chin, Sam had managed: "Hello, I'm calling about the ad?" She pressed her cheek into the cold metal of the pay phone box.

"What are your qualifications?"

The ad had given no clear indication of what she was applying for.

Should she talk about her other jobs? For years, she'd worked six nights a week at the pharmacy in her foster parents' neighborhood. La Princesa de la Farmacia, her aunt called her when Sam saw her at mass. It was a joke and a dig; she knew enough to know that if she reacted to it as either, she would be reacting the wrong way.

"Hello? Gringa? You want a job or not?" A snap of gum clicked in Sam's ear.

"I can lift fifty pounds, organize merchandise, and deal with customers." A short, sharp laugh pushed out of the receiver and then died so suddenly Sam wasn't sure she'd heard it at all.

"Fine. You at the university? Be at the commuter lot at 6am tomorrow."

The line went dead. No talk of pay or hours.

~

Sam didn't mind being on food. Food was technically the kitchen, any freezers in the house, and sometimes, if the place was huge, a pantry. She had a black bin for perishables, a blue bin for canned goods, and a white bin for reusables (plates and cups, dish towels and cutlery). Back at the office, which was really the basement of a building somewhere in the next town, all of the items were sorted and sent away: to Goodwill, to shelters and food banks, posted on Ebay and sold to antique dealers upstate. Maybe sold to Hollywood and used as props; who really knew?

"Never take anything, even a cracker, from the houses for yourself." Marina told her the first day, once in Spanish, once in English.

Soon Sam found out that everyone takes something from the houses.

"All of the things left behind look lonely, don't they?" Mel had asked her, a few days ago, tucking a silver coin set into her huge pockets. Sam knew that loneliness wasn't really the reason. People take because they've lost something. Want something in return.

Today, Sam clears pantry shelves sticky with years of dust, taking each item away from where it lived. She erases them from the landscape of this life. She does this in her photographs, or tries to. Evoke absence, emptiness: the lack of sigh on skin, press of palm to shoulder, mop of brow.

"It's all so abstract," her professor said first semester, looking at her photographs of blank walls. "How can you make the viewer feel an absence? What's not there, without photographing nothing?"

Sam does not know the answer to this question. Not yet. She knows that her existence is built around this absence, and for her whole life, she's tried to explain it herself: it's like building the center of a jigsaw puzzle with no border, no edge pieces to tell her where this or that piece should come in, where she would fit in the entire scheme of her life.

For now, she looks to other people's lives, anything that might give her a clue, might tell her what the familiar thing was that's not there anymore. She steals the details of kitchens and cupboards, tells herself stories about the people who are gone, tries to translate this into pictures that have no subject.

~

Her foster parents tried to give her a scheme, to show her through jobs and church and responsibility that she wasn't floating, untethered. Ward of the state was a whispered term in her childhood world. But it's all she's ever felt she was, even after she started going to mass with her aunt, her birth mother's sister, who wrote her letters for years, letters she finally decided to answer.

These are the things that she eventually knows about her birth mother: that she came from Colombia, that she had married an Italian, that she spoke no English, that she loved clothes, that she went insane and gave her up. *How do you go insane?* Sam will wonder, much later, after she finds out what she wants to know. Do you lean and lean into it, the tree of your spine bending into the wind until you break? For now, she searches among the belongings of the dead for anything that feels familiar, for a face that will speak to her, that will cause her stomach to drop with recognition. Won't her body know its mother? Isn't it instinct that calls animals to their kin in the wild, that thing that's called belonging?

"You are a freak of nature, you know that?" Andrea, her roommate, had been astounded that Sam had no pictures, no posters, only a map of the world tacked beside her bed. When she couldn't sleep at night Sam sat in front of the map and in the darkness traced her finger along the creased paper until she found a spot she thought must be it. Where she belonged. Not necessarily where she was going to or had been. Or possibly both of those things.

"I'm unfettered." Sam had answered. It is easy to sound coy, cool, sly, all the things she didn't feel inside. It is easy to try on masks when you're never sure which one is actually you.

As parents drop their kids off early so that they can get some studying, partying, socializing done before the term starts back up, Sam sits under the elms and reads books and watches. She had been lucky to get into this school, lucky to have been able to get away from the city she was brought up in, the eyes of the people who knew who and what she was and didn't let her forget it. Their stares and too-kind smiles didn't let her forget it. She hasn't bothered to tell her foster parents about her job, her photos; she is 18 now and though they said she would always be welcome in their home, they never officially adopted her. They would have lost their monthly checks from the state for her safekeeping. So she belongs to no one. The door to her childhood closes and she lets it.

She doesn't want to be between those two worlds anymore.

∽

"You'll need to be careful with the pictures," Marina says.

Mel, who usually handles books and photographs, anything that can be resold to used bookstores or antique shops' instant ancestor bins in Rhinebeck, has come down with something.

Sam nods towards several cartons on the floor: "In those?"

"Pictures in the smaller ones, and be neat. Books stacked in the larger." There is a thud from the front room, a dropped end table, or worse. "When you're done in here, do a wall sweep, and then help drag the trash out to the curb."

Marina sweeps down the hall, leaving Sam in the family room, the air stained ochre by the sun seeping through the heavy raffia drapes. They are supposed to keep all curtains, doors, windows closed; it is a private matter, what they are doing. No one's business but the bereaved.

She rummages through the books, finding Nora Roberts, Stephen King, other popular writers found in any drugstore. Nothing that she was interested in, though there were some receipts stuck in among the pages that she'd give to Marina just in case they were important to the bereaved. This is what you called someone who lost someone else. Am I bereaved? She wonders. Should I be?

She sits cross-legged on the floor and piles the albums around her, slowly peeling back the cellophane that keeps them in place and unsticking someone else's memories from the tacky paper. She does this slowly and methodically, careful to keep her fingerprints off the cracking ink of the Polaroids.

Each album is a story that she tries to figure out. She searches for clues as to who is who, and when there are no names or dates scrawled on the back, she guesses. James and Juanita, Texas 1982. Like that. It is a game she is spending too much time on, a game that will probably get her fired. Sam keeps telling herself that she isn't going to take them. Even if they fall out of the photo box as they are packing up the van and she sticks them in her pocket, she'll give them back. Instead, she carefully chooses a stack, sticks them under her thigh as she sits on the floor, and at the end of the day, tucks them in her bra.

"We got everything?" Marina raises her eyebrows, tattooed on, like her eyeliner and lipstick so that even early in the morning, when she picks Sam up in the campus commuter lot, she looks like she's done more than roll off of her mattress and into whatever clothes line the floor in front of her bed.

"Yeah, looks like it." When she was very young, Sam had learned not to fidget when she lied. When you moved, they could see you were nervous, that you had something to hide. When someone did something bad, a social worker came to check and definitely wasn't taking you with her at the end of the visit. Or if she did, it wasn't anywhere better than where you were. Better to keep very still.

Marina hesitates for a moment. Looks at Sam. And then, "I'll lock up, you close the trunk."

Sam never steals from the van. Once it's out of the house it belongs to Marina and you don't steal from your boss. It is a rule she makes up and she will break it, of course, over and over through the course of her life, but isn't it something to know that starting out, she intended to be good?

Beneath her shirt, the photos curve around her upper rib cage, her breast, the heavy paper protective, an absurd illicit armor, and as clunkily obvious, like a gun under her arm. Marina lets her off at the traffic light in town; she is late for an appointment and Sam says she doesn't mind the walk.

"Don't leave without your money." Marina shoves a small wad of bills through the open car window.

"Thanks. I'll see you next week?" Sam does not count the money, just shoves it into her pocket.

"I'll call if I need you." Marina's eyes are tired and night dark, like Sam's. You could be my mother, Sam thinks then, for the first time.

∼

Sam slips through the heavy wooden door of the dorm and makes her way to the third floor. Andrea isn't there, and she is glad. She slides the photos out of her bra; the warmth of her body is held in them for a moment, then quickly fades. She lays them out on her bed, the black cotton of the comforter providing a stark background, a frame for the moments of lives she now possesses but has no context for.

It feels a little like watching a movie you've never seen with the sound turned off, the scenes out of order: you never know the plot, never know the characters' voices. Brown tables, elbows, a mouth bending over a birthday, wedding, anniversary cake. A bit of curtain. Or wedding dress. You see snippets of lives and everything that can be captured in fragments, moments. All you will ever get are the moments, superimposed over the image you had in your head, the one that was empty just moments before.

Sam slides each picture around her bed. Arranging and rearranging them like a memory game she will never win. When she tires of this, she leaves them on the bed, strips off her work clothes, pulls on a fresh pair of jeans and a t-shirt. Soon Andrea will be back and they will walk up the hill toward the dining hall. Watch students slide on cafeteria trays down the other side, bellies pressed to the ground, their mouths smoking and laughing, sound drowned into coffee cups filched from the dining room. Sam will tell Andrea about her family, show her the pictures.

DISAPPEARER

D ori is conjuring her sister. Her supplies: a tape deck ready to play, a long teaspoon for stirring the instant coffee, a swatch she cut off the couch before she left home the first time, and of course the TV, which is the conduit for everything. The show, Taxi, has been off the air since 1983, though was alive in reruns through the early 90s at least. She remembers sitting on the edge of the orange and brown plaid couch while her sister, Erin, punched the numbers on the box-like remote, waiting for the theme-song to come bursting through the sides of the Zenith. In her memories, it is always late in the afternoon, after school but before any adults come home, even before her mother, who works second shift at the restaurant only sometimes, sits chain-smoking and drinking tall glass after tall glass of brandy-laced iced coffee at the kitchen counter. Of course, if Dori and Erin are watching Taxi, it was ages before they decided to go to the edge of the river.

If Dori can make Taxi come back, it will fix everything; it will maybe even fix her. That's what spells are supposed to be: a fix. A guarantee that if you have all the ingredients, everything it once took to make something real, all the hundreds of bones and feathers in a black bird or all the nuts and bolts and grease and smoke in a car, you can make that thing the way it was: true and happening, and just the way you remember it. Of course, nothing is ever just the way you remember it being. There's always something you forgot to remember that pricks into existence at the last minute that makes it not as great as you remember after all. But that's ok. It's ok if it's not perfect. Dori's got pieces of everything that made the past the past and she hopes that will be enough, even for it to be the way it was for a moment. A moment is all she needs.

Her life is divided (and maybe it always was), into before Erin and after. Right after Erin left (or was taken, or disappeared), Dori felt like she was the only person who remembered her. Sometimes she felt like she was on one side of a bridge and everyone else was on another. Her mother, Erin's boyfriend, the police, they all wanted her to cross over, to move on and act like Erin had never existed, to forget. But Dori couldn't. Do you forget someone just because they're dead? Or gone? Do they forget you? Dori knew that it was painful to remember, and that's maybe why her life ended up that way it did.

∽

"We out of coffee again?" Strummer fixed her with his one brown eye, shaking the obviously empty coffee can at the floor. He was used to Dori drinking up all the caffeine in the house, stealing his speed. She usually scrawled IOUs in black eyeliner on the mirror, the stove, his headboard.

"Tony Danza marathon," Dori answered, chewed fingertip tapping the scratched laminate.

There was a creak from the bedroom, the sigh of ancient bed springs, a flump from a pile of pillows. It could have been a cat but it wasn't.

It was okay, though. Dori didn't mind other girls in the apartment.

Strummer nodded and slipped on a pair of decaying Vans, grabbed a five from the jar marked "drug money" that sat on the top of the fridge, and headed out the door. Dori knew he was only going to the store but she started imagining what it would be like if he never came back. She decided that she didn't care that much. Not really.

~

Here's how Dori rediscovered that she could conjure things. One night, she succeeded in calling Taxi up from vaults of the TV station basement (where all good shows went to die). She was very drunk. Not fall-down-vomit drunk, like she got when she drank wine. The kind of drunk that comes from taking one shot of tequila every half hour all day long. She could feel the equilibrium of blood to alcohol to sweat in her body. Everything was completely balanced in that everything, her heart lungs liver were saturated and equal and now she could exist in the magic place between wakefulness and dream and intoxicated and totally fucked up.

No one else was home; they were either still at the party or passed out in the street or on the subway somewhere. Lots of kids lived here in the factory, trying to be artists but really being too drunk and high most of the time to create anything. Dori was sitting on the floor beside the television, trying to remember the thing that is always in her head, the song she had been trying to remember for years. She simply started chanting "taxitaxitaxi" long and slow like the best kisses, the plosiveness of tee and ex popping on her tongue, and then through the magic of tequila and wishes the theme song came to her, she hummed it loud against the side of the TV, its electric heat pressed to her cheek. She could see herself on the couch in front of her, sitting in the exact same spot as she always had when Erin was around; the girl on the couch is already almost 16, her life already on its way to wrong. She had forgotten that she was full of magic back then. That she could make things happen, appear and disappear. But soon after then, that special time when magic lit her limbic system without her even trying, her days were taken up with blotting everything out with Jim Beam and her nights were ringed with the blue smoke of Parliaments and the memory of Erin was already almost gone, fading out like a program the antenna of her mind couldn't quite grasp onto, couldn't quite pierce with its skinny aluminum body. The show only came back on that night for a minute or two before the electric flickered off because no one bothered to pay the electric bill again, but Dori knew what she'd done.

∽

Erin had loved Taxi. She loved that it was a way station, a port from which all the characters came and went and if they wanted to they always had a car ready to take them across one of the million New York bridges and from there, anywhere. Erin was always telling Dori that everything was a bridge, even Erin was a bridge, something Dori had to cross to get to the rest of her life. The characters on Taxi reminded her of that, she said. People who were just searching and trying not to be stuck on one side or the other. Erin said:

—They're like people we could know, you know? In New York, you could find anyone.

Dori liked Taxi for the oddballs, of course, people that she thought she'd never know, like Latka and the Reverend. But Dori also drank jar after jar of pickle juice, licked freshly mown grass (for the taste-smell), and flushed her mother's cigarettes sometimes. Dori lived weird. When she was almost grown-up a boy she was sleeping with would tell her that she was just five degrees off of everything, which threw the whole world off kilter into outer space.

∼

Dori knew another spell that her life had proven true: if you stopped thinking about someone, anyone, from the man who begged for change at the truck stop (Jesus H. Christ, her mother would say, get a job, as she shifted her skinny freckled legs in their wooden platform sandals), to the neighbor's dog (which was fine because Dori hated dogs), to your best friend, to the man with the blank face that she wasn't supposed to talk about, they would disappear. You wouldn't notice at first—they'd get grey around the edges and then you wouldn't see them so often, though really you wouldn't think about it, because you were in the process of forgetting already, the process of erasing them; they would go away, bit by bit by bit until one day they weren't there anymore and maybe you wouldn't even notice. This happened a lot. After Dori and Erin and their mom moved across the river the first time, Dori's best neighborhood friend forgot to send postcards or call when her mom was drunk-asleep and soon even the friend's face started to disappear in Dori's dreams, a big blank question-mark of a spot, like the bottom of a worn shoe whose size has been sweated away and then after a while Dori's mother said: Who? when Dori asked if they could take a trip across the river to visit, like the friend never existed at all.

Erin was the first one to prove that this spell worked. Everyone (Erin's sweet-dumb boyfriend, who had been the meat-packer at the Grand Union until he was fired under suspicion of murder and kidnapping and lots of other things; her mother who just smoked and drank until she pickled and ashed herself when Dori was 17; and maybe even the blank-faced man) pretty much forgot Erin until one day she was just gone for good. But that's getting ahead. The spell worked loads of times before that.

≈

One time when Dori and Erin were bored, or maybe just fed up with the adults in their lives, they tried to cast a disappearing spell. It was September summer, early Fall, maybe-Winter-would-never-come kind of weather

—The den closet. I'll keep the door closed and hide behind the coats if anyone but you tries to find me.

Erin had clearly thought this through. Erin always knew all the answers to everything.

—What about going to the bathroom? And eating? I could probably only sneak you candy.

Dori was clunky-clumsy then, didn't know how to move her

already-woman's hips so that they didn't bang into walls and corners and startle the people she was trying to slink away from.

—You could sneak me a four-course meal, dweeb. No one is ever going to know. And I can go in the middle of the night when no one is awake.

Their mother almost never slept at night unless she was really drunk, so this was a risky proposition, but Dori thought it might be fun to sneak things to the closet and pretend she knew nothing. Her most important job, they decided, was going to be to make sure Erin didn't run out of cassettes or batteries. Erin had won one of those new Walkman players for selling the most subscriptions to the Reader's Digest or something. Erin was good at making the things she wanted appear, just like that. Dori suspected that she was just as good at disappearing things, too. Dori was extremely jealous of this ability but always agreed to help with whatever Erin wanted to do anyway because really, she loved Erin and there was nothing else to do. They hadn't known about the river's edge or met the blank-faced man yet.

Dori was glad she wasn't casting the spell, only helping. She was terrified of the closet. There was a mirror on the back, and once, when Erin was angry at Dori for something, she pushed Dori inside and sat with her back against the door and wouldn't let Dori out until she chanted Bloody Mary Bloody Mary Bloody Mary in front of the mirror. Dori was extra scared because she knew that Bloody Mary came from mirrors. You only had to call her and she would come, just like that.

—Keep going! Erin said, her back heavy against the door. Don't stop until you feel her stinking breath on your neck.

Dori wanted to stop but she knew she couldn't or else Erin would never let her out. She sucked in breath after breath between hiccoughing out Bloody Mary's name until someone wrenched the door open and screamed at her:

—Who the hell are you talking to? It was their mother. She had a cigarette that was mostly ash, dangling from the filter like one of those impressions of bodies from Pompeii, the ones that looked like they would collapse if you breathed on them.

—Erin. Dori said. She locked me in and made me—

—Jesus H. Christ. Stop talking to yourself all the time. Her mother slammed the closet door but it only bounced back, Dori's reflection coming fast towards her then quickly away again, like there were two of her moving at completely different speeds.

Erin never stayed mad at Dori for long, though, and that's why Dori couldn't stay mad at her either. She would always help Erin, no matter what. Especially when she wanted to do magic—disappearing and appearing and other spells.

In the end, they almost won, almost made Erin utterly and completely disappear. They would have totally won but it was Easter, the only only time their mother made them dress in one of their pale plaid dresses that hadn't even fit last year and go to church. When their mother couldn't find them, she stood in the kitchen with the fish-limp dress hanging by its faded tag off the hook of a metal hanger and she screamed until Dori felt like her ears were bleeding. It wasn't clear to Dori until much later that their mother had completely forgotten about them and had been on her way out the door until she realized she couldn't very well show up to Easter church alone. How would that look? At the time, Dori was more worried about what their mother would do to them, especially since she'd threatened no more TV ever if Dori didn't reveal her secret hiding place. Dori thought about this hard, her too-small dress cutting into her ribs (the black velvet one that her mother was always calling morbid and trying to throw away) and making it hard to breathe, until, finally, she was forced to open the closet door, the mirror catching the early light and making copies of all of them, the reflection in the cheap glass showing several mothers and Erins and Dories.

—This is where you've been? Jesus H. Christ. Take that goddamn morbid thing off and get your ass to church. Their mother shook the dress, making its mothball smell dance with dust particles in dim light of the closet.

Erin shrugged and pushed herself up off the floor. She pressed past both Dori and their mother and instead of going out the front door, climbed out the window. Dori knew Erin was going to go find her boyfriend, who was probably aching for her, positively pining after so many minutes and hours and days without her (Dori learned the words aching and pining from the romance books she stole from the library; she tried to remember them and use them in everyday conversation so she wouldn't forget).

Their mother gripped the dress in her fists. Dori followed her into the kitchen and watched as she threw it on the kitchen floor and then muttered:

—You don't appreciate anything. That's why we can't do anything nice.

Then she swirled dark rum into her coffee glass, threw it back, and slammed out to her car and then probably to the Church. The dress stayed on the floor for weeks, deflating into the linoleum until it was almost flat and Dori almost didn't have to step over it. While the dress was being disappeared by being ignored, Erin was disappeared by being forgotten like this, over and over and over. Sometimes Dori would talk to Erin and their mother would tell her to knock it off, which also didn't help Erin stick around. Their mother never really understood Erin, anyway. Never really loved her. At least, Dori didn't think so. Erin hadn't ever seemed to care about that though.

Dori was like the dress: not so much forgotten as ignored. She could read her stolen romance novels and secret magic books and comics and sit in trees and be the one that was remembered at supper time, at bedtime, whenever she did something just five degrees off of everyone else. The only time she wasn't ignored was after Erin was truly gone for good and then the police questioned her but it was too late and they didn't believe her anyway.

～

When Dori told Erin's boyfriend what had really happened, he asked her this: Are you crazy or something??

What could Dori say that she hadn't said already?

Dori didn't think she was crazy. She didn't even think the blank-faced man was crazy with his skiff and robe and bag of coins. She hadn't even known what was in the bag until the third or fourth or fifth time that Erin had dragged her into the weeds, their sickly green and skinny-sharp razor bodies cutting her shins as they skulked along the river's edge.

Nothing had really happened before that. Erin would stand there and just wait, while Dori got bored and started to imagine decaying fingers of people who'd been murdered or the slimy sharp mouths of crocodiles in the river. The last time they went together, she'd just about convinced herself that an enormous croc was about the jump out of the water and eat her when she felt Erin press against her.

—Be quiet. Erin had breathed, her words clammy against Dori's neck. Watch.

Dori watched and for a long time she didn't see anything. It was the middle of the morning but somehow clouds came or maybe the sun went down and suddenly it was twilight and the torn lip of a low skiff appeared out of the reeds and the water. In the skiff was a figure who Dori thought was a Jedi maybe but the robes hid everything until he turned toward them and there was nothing in his face that she could see (so not a Jedi, not a real one like Obi Wan Kenobi). No eyes or mouth or anything human. Nevertheless, the robed figure (who over time, minutes, hours, became a man, a man with features and hands but still had nothing in his face, a blank screen) looked at them and held out his hand and Erin leaned over the water, her body suddenly skinny and sharp like the razor weeds and would have gone to him then but Dori held her arm tight tight in her small brown fists with their sharp sharp nails.

—You're hurting me, Erin said.

Dori felt Erin's skin break away from her own and she knew she couldn't stop Erin. Not now. Maybe not ever. Erin waded through the murk until she was up to her thighs in the river. The water made it look like Erin was bleeding but that was only because her skirt was red. Now it was red and wet. The blank-faced man grasped Erin's chin very lightly, like he was holding a ripe plum and was worried he'd bruise its sensitive skin.

Dori wanted to scream but couldn't: when she saw the blank-faced man (he was so grey, his robes covered everything about him) she thought she might never breathe again.

Erin opened her mouth and held out her tongue. There was a gold coin on it, the twilight caught it like it was an early star, and suddenly her mouth was full of light. Dori wondered if Erin had swallowed the sky.

—You shall pass. The blank-faced man said, or maybe only thought. It was hard to say. His mouth wasn't moving at all, but Dori definitely heard, or maybe just knew he said it. Maybe it was a trick, like ventriloquism. The blank-faced man plucked the coin from Erin's mouth and placed it in his bag.

All the light in the world flicked off.

～

I'm going to show you a trick, Erin said.

Erin's clothes clashed brilliantly with the orange and plaid couch. She was wearing one of their mother's Stevie Nicks skirts and a sparkly scarf, all broomstick witchy. A bruja, her father would have said, if he'd still been alive. It had been such a long time since anyone had seen him; Dori just assumed he was dead at that point. She couldn't even remember what he had looked like or even what he wore. She couldn't have remembered him back, even if she had wanted to. Which she never did.

—I'm wearing an orange and plaid couch suit, Erin commanded. Even my face and neck are covered in itchy fabric.

Dori tried not to giggle, even though her stomach felt giddy. She didn't want to break the spell that Erin wanted her to believe in.

Close your eyes and count to 11, Erin whispered, making her voice fade slowly like a warm breeze snaking through the tops of trees. When you open your eyes I'll be gone. Eventually you'll forget me completely; it will be like I never existed.

Dori completely believed this was possible because she loved Erin and knew that magic worked and if you stopped seeing, whatever you didn't see would just disappear. She knew this, too, because she would lay in her bed at night and make herself stop seeing the blank-faced man, his hands, his bag of coins. She stopped seeing the flash of metal on Erin's tongue, Erin's fingers in his palm, the sparkle of money dropping into his fist.

But Dori didn't get to 11 because her mother came in screaming about how her car was missing again and if Dori knew anything about it and wasn't telling she'd beat her with her espadrille shoe. She sounded ridiculous but Dori tried not to laugh. She even kept her eyes closed so she wouldn't have to break the spell, wouldn't have to see her mother crazy angry. And when she opened her eyes, Erin was gone.

～

They found the car two weeks later at the edge of the river. Erin had been hiding since the morning with the couch. Dori knew she was still around because at night Erin would sit on the end of her bed and tell her stories about the places she hid and the secret things people did all day when they thought no one was watching. Dori would turn her face to the opposite wall and look out of the corner of her eye toward the window and see Erin reflected there: a wisp of blond, a sparkle, a sneer. Dori stopped being able to see Erin, though, once her boyfriend pressed his face up against the window looking for her. After that she could only hear Erin, though she had to listen very hard. After a while, Dori kept falling asleep during their visits and in the morning could not always remember what was said. Eventually, Erin stopped coming because Dori stopped remembering to look for her. At first, Dori thought that maybe Erin had found their father and would never come back. She hated Erin for that, and sometimes even tried to forget she had even existed. Their mother didn't even care that Erin was gone, though she'd stopped yelling at Dori for mumbling to herself, one of their mother's pet peeves, which was something.

～

—One more time. The cop said. What did the man in the boat do to you?

Dori had already told them everything.

—Not to me, she said. To my sister.

—Your sister.

The cop looked at her mother, who was frowning at the floor and massaging the bridge of her nose.

—Yes. She got all wet walking through the river to the boat. She gave the man her coin. I didn't want her to go. But he grabbed her face and then she started glowing and then ...

—Goddamnit, her mother interrupted. What the hell happened to my car?

—Erin—Dori started to explain, how she'd made her come with

her, how the car would be faster, how with it they'd be back before their mother even woke up, how they'd cross the bridge and back and go wherever they wanted and maybe even never come back, they'd be escape artists, disappearers.

Dori's mother stood up and reached over the desk, grabbed Dori's chin hard. Not like the blank-faced man had. Not like she was a ripe fruit, a sensitive plum.

—I don't want to hear that name ever again. Her mother whispered.

Dori was so frightened that she agreed. She never mentioned Erin to her mother again. She tried not to even think about her.

～

Dori feels bad about that now. She thinks that Erin would have come back for good if only Dori had remembered to think about her more, to talk to her more, even if she couldn't quite see the wisps of her hair reflected in the window. It was just that it was hard. After the thing with Erin and the car, her mom had been down on her for being just five degrees off a lot and she wasn't even allowed to climb trees or walk to the Grand Union by herself. Not that it stopped her. Dori became a trickster after Erin left, stealing rides with strangers and drinking behind the school with older boys. She even tried to bleach her hair so it would look like Erin's, but because it was so dark naturally, it just came out orange. Eventually, she figured out how to make it perfectly white, bleached out and spiked like the punkers on TV, like the bird and fish and other animal bones down at the river's edge. She still did all the things she had always done—drank pickle juice and spent spare moments in the tops of trees reading her stolen books—but now she did all the things that Erin had done, or had always wanted to do.

Dori stopped waiting for Erin's boyfriend to show up at their bedroom window and started waiting for him at work. Erin's boyfriend's hands were like long, thin cuts of roast beef, cracked from running the slicer and light pink where his callouses split in the winter. They were warm and soft like good meat, too. Dori would press her cheek against the cool metal of the walk-in freezer at the Grand Union and when she felt the cold of the wall and the hot of his body at the same time, she imagined kisses light like the touch of a flower beneath her chin.

∼

It took Dori a long time to remember Erin's forgetting spell (count to 11 and close your eyes) and an even longer time to remember, to know that she could conjure things, that she could make tv shows just happen from blank snowy screens and maybe other things by thinking about them, by crossing the bridges in her memory, back to where things started, where instead of being just one girl alone inside and out, there were two: the girl she really was, and the girl, her sister, that she loved.

∼

The second time Dori conjured Taxi, she was walking in Times Square, back when it was dirty all the time, with some guy who wasn't her boyfriend at all but was pretending to be and she was trying very hard to make him go away but she needed money so she decided to bring him back to Queens (where she'd been living with a bunch of other girls and guys who brought their dates home a lot, who all seemed to wear the same clothes and push the same grunts and gasps from their throats instead of talking). At that moment, Dori missed Erin so fiercely, so completely that the TVs that lined the shop window she was leaning on, trying to ignore her not-boyfriend, flickered on and there it was: Taxi. She stared and stared and still couldn't believe it. It stayed on for hours and Dori just stood there, watching and she even thought that maybe the girl that was standing behind her in the window, almost right where she stood with the bleach-blond hair and the sneer and crucifix dangling for fashion only was really Erin. Erin who before she had disappeared made life better, made life magic, made spells and wove stories that made all of the bad, scary things ok.

Erin, she whispered, ErinErinErin.

But perhaps her voice was too soft, her mind too awake for conjuring. Perhaps her magic wasn't powerful enough. She'd practiced as often as she could since the night when she'd pressed her cheek to the heat of the metal television box and chanted taxitaxitaxitaxi until she almost huffed herself out. Almost every time, the show would come on and so Dori hoped that she could make Erin really be there, could remember her back. She decided that she was going to just stand here until she could actually feel Erin's skin beside her again and then she would turn around and they would go home to her apartment in Queens together.

She must have fallen asleep waiting for Erin to materialize completely because the cop and the store manager were yelling way too loud:

—Miss? Miss? You gotta move. You can't just stand here all night. I gotta store to run.

Dori didn't want to open her eyes or turn around or leave because she knew that by falling asleep she had broken the spell.

—What channel are they on? What channel? Dori's voice sounded strange to her, blond and sneering and it didn't belong to her anymore. It was like she was someone else now. Someone she was just remembering.

—TVs been off for hours, the store manager said. Off since the Late Late Show.

His voice was full of water, of rivers, bridges; it was drowning and she couldn't grab hold.

—What channel? What channel? Dori could feel the cop and manager look at each other even though she didn't have her eyes open, not yet. She had to remember first. To really remember all of it. Everything that happened that September summer. The river, the river.

—Seven. It was channel seven.

When Dori got home, she dragged the old black and white portable into her room to try again while her roommates were sleeping but no matter what she did, channel seven was only static, black and white water pushing violently against the glass of the screen, like it hadn't been on ever, like it couldn't remember that it was a station that was supposed to play.

~

The TV she has now is color, which she hopes won't interfere with her spell. Since she moved in with Strummer, close to the edge of the river, she's successfully reappeared many things: the friend's cat Dori lost while she was stoned, her mother's beat-up Dodge Dart that she either left in Tucson or was stolen, and now, maybe hopefully Erin. She knows that now the smaller things are accomplished (since leaving New York for good, she has spent so much time training her mind, making small things happen), Erin will be a piece of cake.

To prepare she digs out her and Erin's old cassettes, the flashlight (which only worked that one September summer, the summer Erin disappeared), and a pile of batteries. She turns on the tape deck (it was a Walkman, yes, she knows, but she thinks inaccuracy can be forgiven here, because the sounds and pictures need space to move, roam, gel together into an Erin form in her living room). She turns on the TV (MTV isn't MTV anymore, no, no all-the-time videos or remote control game shows, but it's still the same channel, yes still the same number on the big black box). She spreads the cigarettes and brandy-iced coffee and a smooth piece of the orange and plaid couch, moldering with her in this basement by the water's edge, where nothing moved or really lived in so so long.

But she can't think about that yet. She's got to make Erin real again, and all the things that Dori has done and become can disappear, float away in the static snow of the TV screen.

THE DEVOURING

A DREAM BETWEEN TWO RIVERS

Brasil

I first saw her where the two rivers meet, brown and black, pressing their long, watery bodies together over mud and sand. The others were snoring in their slatted seats or gazing with glazed eyes at the earth-colored heads of the capybara poking through the great, green-bladed shore.

Her body seemed like a log bleached by the hot Brazilian sun, an inlet of the light water of the white Amazon River that had slipped into the Rio Negro. But as she passed close to the boat, I saw her irises: black-blue rimming bright green, the jungle canopy contained by the night sky. These colors undulated—the belly of that forest floor sliding along the arms, the legs of the trees, shaking them until bouquets of leaves were flung away.

I blinked.

And the seam where the black and white rivers held one another was again clean, a blank, snaking line. Soon we were crossing over it, the wooden bottom of the boat sliding through the black river to the shore on its bank.

Cambridge

Justine's eyes were like cornflowers, dull and flat and hard blue, with nothing behind them but present everywhere: in the sky, in street signs, in the weave of the patchy scarves on winter city sidewalks or the hair of students who wandered across the river from MassArt. And of course, in almost every variety of local wildflower that pushed through the cracks of city streets. After she left, I was so desperately alone, surrounded by a sea of blue that both rejected yet wouldn't leave me be, wouldn't let me heal.

So it was safer to spend my hours at the Herbarium, caring for our collection of rare and dangerous blooms. Orchids are my specialty— their bodies so fragile, yet so resilient. Their blooms, both sharp and soft, their nectars, and even their perfumes and petals, sweet and deadly poisonous. They can protect themselves while remaining entirely serene. And of course, their colors are vibrant, bright. Warm against the dead memories of cornflower blue.

Brasil

The thrush of small furred legs cutting through the blade grass preceded our small group into the jungle. We set camp on opposite edges of a clearing, saying little before we dispersed to collect what we came for. I knew none of them well; even on an orchid hunt, evolutionary botanists tend to stick to plants and our talk skims only the skin of exterior, personal life. Anything else is too dangerous. Justine, wherever she is now, helped me understand that: the flesh of the flower is much safer than the flesh of the friend, the lover. Even if the flower is full of poison, you can appreciate its beauty without being caught in it, without being snared by it. Flowers don't have eyes.

Cambridge

My orchids were nothing to Justine, and whenever I had tried to explain their perfectly balanced sensuality to her, she'd simply bite my lips closed with her even white teeth. She was too hard, too unforgiving, too cornflower blue. When we made love (but was it love? Justine would have said we were just fucking) she was so hard. Her body was a stone, one that I felt on my stomach, my neck, my heart. Even so, when she smashed my rare orchids and corpse flowers (with the absurdly phallic stamen that we had giggled over when she could coax a few drinks into me) over the sink in lieu of a goodbye note, I felt as though she sliced me open and dug out my core. I was empty now, alone. Even the heavy weight of being bound is sometimes a comfort.

Brasil

I found nothing but *Cattleya intermedia* orchids that first day, pale violet and small, not much different than you'd find in a well-kept garden back home. I was looking for something rarer, something sharp and new that I could take back to the lab, dissect, grow, and care for, whose poison I could bottle up and somehow inject into my soul, inoculating myself against the temptations and impatience of lesser flowers. Of course, everyone else was looking for it, too. The Carrion Bride, rather absurdly and affectionately called, their white hoods gaudy with fringed bloom and their throats red with the blood of their prey, were beyond rare, a true flesh-eating orchid. And thought by indigenous tribes to cure blood ailments, even cancer, before it was hunted to near-extinction by Victorian orchid hunters. Which was, of course, why this trip was so important. My body was already dripping with sweat, my face and hands smeared with mud, but I hardly cared. It was an escape. It was what I needed. It's what we all need. To be surrounded by the green and black and absurdly painted flowers.

At night, there is no escape. No matter how tired I am, or how sore and bloody my fingers are from cutting specimens from trees, I dream about Justine. Her irises haunt me, spill from the corners of her deep eyes onto her skin, seeping into her hair, running down her neck, her breasts, until she is painted the darkest shade of blue I'd ever seen, her entire body transforming into a freezing sea, until her cold blue calculating eyes are all that she is and I know I will drown in her. I could drown in her right now and never escape these dreams.

Cambridge

"I can't fucking believe you."

She stalked around the apartment, bottle in hand.

I stood in the doorway, palms pressed against the jamb on either side of me, as if bracing for an earthquake. I laughed. A nervous tic I'd developed along the way, from my father, or another lover, I think. I'm certain it didn't start with Justine. I'd already been so afraid when I met her. It couldn't have started with Justine.

"You're goddamn leaving? To go pick some fucking flowers? Well, fine. Fine. Just fuck you then."

Was it then that she started throwing my orchids against the walls? The sink? Was that another fight? I can't remember. I know I must have spoken, told her that the expedition was important to me, that it wouldn't leave for months yet, and that I wouldn't be gone that long. I was reasonable and calm. I just don't remember it. I don't remember anything but standing in that doorway, between Justine and the rest of the world. She was so angry. It was a cold night. I remember that but I'm not sure what happened after.

Brasil

Before it becomes too dark and mosquitoes drive us into our tents, under our protective nets, our expedition leader tells stories around the fire.

"She's an angry woman," he starts. "And she's fiercely protective of her jungle, especially her flowers. The patasola: she's beautiful at first, she will look exactly like someone you love, someone you want. She'll lead you deep into the trees, and when you're alone, she'll devour you, sucking your blood until you are a shell, until your empty veins collapse into dust to fertilize her bloody flowers."

Most laugh.

But I wonder what it would be like to be sought after that much, even if it was to enact revenge, rather than to love.

Cambridge

"Remember, you agreed to this."

She'd wound the silky rope around my arms, my legs. She did this when she was especially angry. I thought I'd keep her there by letting myself be bound.

Though I wondered why she felt the need to tie me down, I wouldn't have moved. I would have been like the queen in that old fairy tale, who, when the prince comes to bed her, lies perfectly still while he presses her into the cold stones before the hearth.

I always thought that the author must have left something out, that the prince must have had a warm glance for his lover, or maybe even licked her lips before fastening the gag. But perhaps I'm getting that confused with my own story now.

But when she was inside me, I tried to imagine some warmth, even just the heat of being wanted. I tried and would have kept on, though Justine's fingers were so cold. I almost couldn't feel them. Yes, that's what I remember. Not feeling anything.

Brasil

After many long days of searching with no fruit for our efforts, I collapse in my tent, knowing that Justine will be there once I close my eyes. It's something I've resigned myself to, something that I've come to welcome, even. The Justine of my dreams is different now than the Justine that I knew, and this makes me want her more than I ever did. She's shifted, become darker: a night-thing of the jungle, a cloud of perfume from the flowers I so desperately want to find, that hovers, then settles on top of me as soon as I close my eyes. I feel the weight of her breasts, wet from the river, fall heavy on my ribs. Her palms press into my thighs, she slides against me, and bit by bit I can trace the lines of our bodies, one against the other, light flesh against dark flesh, like the rivers. Her mouth latches around my skin, and her teeth bite uneven red garlands into my pale flesh, down my stomach, between my thighs. And when she looks up at me, her eyes catch me, hold me, jungle and night-sky eyes that never lived in the face of my former lover, and it doesn't stop me from wanting what I can't have, what isn't really here. She is Justine and she isn't. She's a dream between two rivers, white and black.

She holds me open, the bowl of my hips an offering, wide to the night air that lies so heavy around me. And when she slides her warm fingers inside of me, it's like she is pressing the stars that had lain so long, so quiet in the field of my body, the stars that Justine just couldn't see, until each one explodes.

~

In the light of day, her body is anything but a dream-wisp, anything but Justine. I see her (or perhaps she allows me to see her) standing at the edge of our clearing in the late morning light, long after my colleagues, who seem to sleep much less fitfully than I, have left camp for the day.

Her solidity is staggering. Her body plump, breasts fuller than even the most lavish flowers, deep brown nipples peeking out of her flesh, both hard and soft, like figs that are overripe, splitting along their heavy bottoms. The curve of her waist, the slope of her hips, so exaggerated and smooth with flesh and I imagine myself melting, becoming water, beads of hot sweat surfing along her voluptuous body.

Her belly is an oval slung between her hips. My eyes slide down her fleshy thighs, see something that is unclear in the night, in my dreams: her left leg ends just below the knee, a bloody stump that drips crimson into the earth.

The heat, the sun, it must be too much for me. I stagger to my knees, palms pressing myself up from the dirt only to find her gone. Perhaps I have a fever or am simply hallucinating. Perhaps I am going insane. My mind knows that the woman isn't real, couldn't be: she's a myth. Probably created by locals long ago to keep intruders out or by orchid hunters themselves to protect their harvest. I feel the earth tremble beneath me, that black earth reaching towards the blue sky, as I collapse in the clearing. I feel the moist kiss of the soil, the sharp bite of the jungle air, all over my body.

~

My days are spent in a haze of half sleep, under the darkest canopy of the jungle, where neither birds nor frogs sing their throaty songs. The others began to whisper about me, and my boss even asked me once if it wasn't a bad idea for me to go out by myself. This verdant place has more than its share of poisons, he said, most of them we can't even begin to guess at.

It's true that I am pale. That beneath my long sleeves and pants my skin is covered with small pinpricks, the red of blood staying bright instead of crusting into black and then flaking away, like normal scars should do. And it's true that I am tired. That I forget why I am here, what I was trying to escape back home. Was there a lover?

I follow her scent. Each day she leads me deeper, eluding me in this sea of leaf and earth. At night she still comes to me, sometimes she even remains. In my dreams, we are always packing to leave this place, our Carrion Bride orchids in their containers, ready to be shipped back to the lab, when I notice her at the entrance to the clearing—a necklace of huge bleeding flowers draped around her shoulders, dripping down her hips. I turn back to the contained blooms and she disappears, leaving footprints and bloody flowers in her wake.

I follow the trail, eating each fleshy bloom. Soon my body is dark with blood and I find a field of orchids with red, dripping mouths. And she is there. Her brown body envelopes me as we lay down in the sun and she feeds me flower after flower, until I finally sleep.

THICK AS SKIN

S elkies have always been forced to choose: the earth or the sea. It is simple: if you want the sea, you must keep your skin, you must never let anyone take it, and you can only step out of it for a few days at a time if you ever want to be able to fit it back on, wrap in its wet warmth. Eventually you will stop stepping out of your skin; you'll dive deep, swim far.

And what if the earth is what makes you shiver? It seems the more painful path. You must step out of your skin and burn it, forfeit your life in the water and remain on cold, dead, dry land. It is the rule: no one lives between, at least not for long. Eventually everyone chooses who they are. But then, this selkie was never much for rules.

Most selkies are dumb and over-content: they have no idea of what magic is out there, what magic they possess on earth, out of water, and they don't care. They don't listen to the fierce desires in their bones, their bodies. They don't know what power is inside them because they never give in to it. But this selkie knew it the first time she felt it. Knew she wanted to feel it again, as much and as often as she could.

The lad couldn't have been much more than 17, a farmer's boy who'd watched the cows and pigs rut often enough by the way he touched her, his callused thumbs pressed into her hips, his oniony breath licking between her shoulders. And when he cried out, she inhaled the world, brought it into herself: the sand, the rocks, the trembling of the lad, and yes, even the sea and the stars were inside her body. After, she walked among the stone cottages and fields until dawn. She counted the tides and found that her seal skin, which she tied over her shoulders like a great grey cape, did not change, did not shrink or cling against her neck. Her flesh didn't itch to be back inside its fat warmth. That didn't happen, not for many weeks yet. She did not miss it, her ocean body, but felt everything in the sea and on the land was at her command. She was free; she could touch everything. And when she wished it, she could return to the sea. And when she longed for the earth, well, there were always strangers on the strand, and when they appealed to her, when she wanted more than a few days, she would press them to the sand, take them inside her, take the energy that they made together and live on it for as long as she chose.

But you know the story now, don't you? Not that it would make a difference to either of us now, caught as we are, bonded together thick as skin and bone. Thicker even.

∽

It was a bit sad, how confused the traveler seemed. Had she ever looked upon a woman with lust before this? Did she know why she did then? It was sea magic, of course, that convinced her, that wooed her. And don't get all gobsmacked about it: she wanted it after all, didn't she?

～

The selkie had barely asked "What do you think it is?" when the traveler was on top of her. The traveler'd pushed the naked lass to the sand, and held her there, or so she thought. The selkie's hands were already reaching for her shed skin, her under skin still bloody and raw from her transformation, and the traveler's hands stung slowly healing flesh that pulsed after being separated from its warm over-layer of fat and silky-grey.

"You're not going anywhere," the traveler, definitely not native to the island, ground her wool-trousered legs into the naked woman-once-beast and tried to hold her down with fleeced forearms. "You slaughtered that seal, didn't you?" Her mouth tore at the air like a drowning fish, and the selkie, who was getting quite a kick out of the whole enterprise, wanted to laugh. Truly. There wasn't a moment when she'd actually been afraid or wary of the entire business. In fact, her hands were already wrapped around her thick skin (which she'd carelessly dropped while trying a dip in her human flesh, a new kind of swimming that soothed and stoked her at the same time), the thing she had been so careful to keep out of reach of humans, really, of men, for who knows how many years.

The traveler, poor lost lamb, didn't know any better, of course, so she did it: she looked into the selkie's eyes, which were a warm, dark brown, definitely not the eyes of anyone who'd grown up on this island of shale in the middle of the sea, and were more the color of unknown sea depths that trick divers with a subtle burst of underwater light.

"Let me go."

The lilting voice crashed around the traveler and easily confused her, causing her hands to slide from the slippery grey pelt. It would be so simple, the selkie thought, I could so easily lay that slick weight at my side, hold her waist. She'd never had a woman before, and why not, she wondered, lilting at the traveler again.

But those three magic words only made the traveler grip the selkie's vulnerable wrists harder, pushing them above her head into the cold, wet sand. The selkie felt rubber boots pull at her bare, webbed feet— tough land skin skidding over the swollen undersides of her wrists. But she didn't believe for a moment that she was caught.

～

The scientist knew she needed to end it, to complete the capture, but at that moment, she was caught up in the naked woman's eyes. The darkness in them, a deep brown that held no other color but, oh, so many secrets. Later, much later, she'd admit (under duress) that she'd definitely wanted to consume the darkness in those eyes, that it almost stopped her from gaining the upper hand.

～

"How could you?" The traveler's bottom lip was full, pink hardening to blue in the cold wind that whipped the shore. The selkie longed to run her thumb along its softness, to seek out the red that surely lay in that mouth. This traveler woman was so perfect and unsure, sitting on a knife-edge of a moment and instead of taking her advantage and freeing herself, the selkie was bound (for but a moment) by an incredible urge to wrap them both in her grey skin and fall forever into the sea.

Sometimes, even this selkie, so in command of the power of her magical body, is overcome by the power of her desire. As she tilted her mouth up to meet the woman's, she forgot why she was there, why the cold grit of the strand knifed into her skin. That is, until their lips met and the flash of the taser stung her side, with the jagged moon the only witness.

~

Perhaps she'd miscalculated the entire endeavor. She was supposed to be catching the selkie, not the other way round. The fish woman had gotten her with that enchanted breath, that lilting accent, those fucking eyes, so deep and dark.

At least she remembered the skin, at least she wasn't that stupid. Whoever holds the skin, holds the heart of the selkie. Or something like that. The books were mostly poetic nonsense. They'd told her the breath could be overcome by garlic tea (which she'd forgotten) and they hadn't warned her about the eyes. Hypnotic, whirlpools of light and dark, sky and sea and ... she had to get a hold of herself. So she kept her distance for as long as she could, watching the selkie roil and toss through a Thorazine induced sleep that would have made a much larger person nearly comatose.

"More ..."

Occasionally, the sea creature's breath heaved. And the woman, a scientist to the last, watched and waited, clicking off the effects of the drug in her mind, and, after a time, sinking into what she could only describe as marvel, wonder. Eventually she began to imagine, not what physical changes had occurred, how the flesh of this creature had stretched and molded itself, regenerating and sloughing off cells, bones, birthing a new body each time it transformed, but what the selkie's body felt like under the waves, in her sea-home. She dreamed about following the selkie there so many times, of pushing into a world that was volcanically dark with the curved shape of the creature under, then above her, their bodies tumbling and pressing together across a bed of something so slick that sometimes their limbs would slide away from one another, but then would find neck, ribs, even fingertip, and hipbone and mouth and she would cry out, a deep, wringing cry. It was frustrating. And not. In the dream, the selkie kept slipping away; she could never find her whole body, her face. Couldn't trace her mouth or her clavicle with her tongue. She wouldn't stay together for that long. Once she found one piece of the selkie, she would disappear. She would become another part of herself, completely disconnected from the piece that came before. The scientist was so frustrated, in dreams. She wanted to own all of the selkie, for the blue-grey and flesh to be at her fingertips, and beneath the waves. But she could never stay under for long. In dreams, the scientist only had land magic, which never, never worked in the sea.

∿

The selkie opened her eyes: a room with white walls, clear boxes hanging in rows from floor to ceiling, each holding something winged, a wisp or a night bird of some kind. She was strapped to a bed, wrapped in a cotton throw, her skin still raw, but soothed, able to breathe. The traveler was sitting by the cot, facing the window and making notes on a tablet.

"Do you always gallivant naked on the strand?"

The selkie swung her head round to this woman, so straight in her high-backed chair and layers of wool. "And what business is it of yours?"

"You were obviously injured. What would have happened had I not come along, Miss ... ?"

"Lira." The selkie smirked then, holding the name in her mouth like a cat holds a mouse. No one had ever bothered to know her as far as names. Men don't pay attention to the right fairy tales. Those that are about names and power and wishes.

"Well ..." The traveler's face reddened like a summer sunset. She was looking at the selkie now, who, slipping out of her cotton dressing, was stunning, even without her sea-grey skin. More so, even. The traveler was clearly having a hard time pulling herself together. "I'm glad you're awake. I've called the hospital, but there are no beds at the moment. The police ... well, they're busy, though I dare say they'll want to speak with you at some point."

Oh, the traveler's eyes were something else, then! Not full of the songs of tiny stone isles and great green hills beyond, as Lira (let's just continue to call her Lira, shall we?) had come to know during her time on this island. But of lands across the sea. Of course, there were no police on this stony island but she doubted the traveler'd had the luxury of even knowing of the pub phone, the only connection to the police on the mainland, which in all likelihood had been out for months, the stormy season having just ended.

"Do you make it a habit, Miss," Lira held her eyes wide, their lashes wider now than even waking anemones and just as dangerous, "of attacking strange women on the strand and then pulling them into your house and tying them to your bed?" Oh, the traveler paled, the blood running from her cheeks like the sun on an early spring morning on the sea, and Lira could feel her gaze soften, just a touch.

"Not nearly often enough."

Lira breathed then, exhaled salt air and the promises found beneath it in the traveler's direction and yes, finally, the traveler's pupils dilated and her lips turned in and she looked like a child who's been caught out stealing and is waiting to be told what they must do to atone. Had Lira not wanted her so badly, she would almost have missed the strong lass from the strand. She had her now, she knew she did.

"Ah, that may be as it may be. But tell me, where is the skin of that seal?" Lira hadn't forgotten her skin, of course she hadn't. How could she? "Where is it?"

"It's no longer yours. It belongs to she who possesses it …" the traveler stopped speaking then; she was staring too hard, eyes as open as her mouth. There is much in a woman's eyes. The traveler turned away then, yes. But only because it was clear then that the selkie had truly won her, that she was beholden now, and forever.

◈

The scientist shut herself in the Witch's house, a cottage of stone identical to her own, though it had been abandoned many years before. Superstition left it to rot and she'd often gone to it in search of specimens that nested in its thatch, its dark and secret places: strange bats, their deep red, blue, purple pelts native to this rocky island and nowhere else and the subject of intense debate in the science community. That's really why she'd come here. Mostly. She'd remembered tales her Nana had told around the kitchen table: selkies and fairies, women who could be caught and made to stay, no matter what you did, no matter how bad you were at making a go of it. When she died, the scientist found her books, her diaries, her accounts of wooing her grandfather in this remote place. Of course, she'd had to see if it was true. To test the hypothesis. Document the phenomenon. What did she have to lose by a test? Science can be a lonely life, as lonely as you make it.

The hearth was in good shape despite neglect and she set the cast iron pot on it and lit a fire beneath. As the pot warmed, she carefully shed her clothes. Dusk slid in the window and smeared its blue light on her skin; it was freezing and her skin felt seared to her bones. She tipped several vials from the cupboards into the pot, one of them full of her own blood, and slowly fed the heavy seal skin into its black mouth. It was warm and slick, even after so many hours of separation from its body, and had a sulfurous smell, the only thing, perhaps that kept the scientist from fitting it whole onto her own body, molding the blubber to her own skin.

Even so close to the heat of the hearth, her body was rigid and icy and she wondered what it must feel like to be able to choose warmth whenever one wants it. To slip in to heat and comfort, cover one's vulnerabilities with a thick exterior. Fanciful notions, romantic nonsense, but still. She wondered. That was not what she was doing here, she knew. She was commanding warmth. Which is an entirely different thing.

By the time the skin had boiled down to a thick, grey fat, she was nearly dead with cold but she set to wait for it to cool just enough so it wouldn't scald. She wondered what the selkie was doing now, if she was searching for her skin or if she had left for another lover, another beach tryst. She'd read in Nana's books that selkies could stay on land as long as they kept absorbing another's energy. How many men would she meet on the strand? How many women? How far would she go to get what she needed? What she wanted? As far as this, the scientist wondered as she smeared the hot grey fat all over her, as far as this?

∼

Of course, Lira knew what was happening by this time, didn't she? Really, one could say she'd expected it all along. As soon as the traveler came back through the door that night, Lira knew she was hers, knew what spells had been wrought. The traveler's eyes were wide and haunted, as if she'd finally surrendered to selkie wiles, the yearning that Lira stirred in her. The traveler, she was so still, as if in a trance, poor darling, caught by the evil witch in a fairy tale without even knowing it. But Lira made it good, didn't she? She stood in the center of the cottage, surrounded by white walls and night wisps, her skin smooth from earlier ministrations but aching just the same. She could feel the traveler's pulse jump as Lira unzipped her trousers, reached to unpick buttons, one by one and when Lira's mouth touched the skin of her belly, oh, it burned, it burned, the fire on sea-flesh stoked up, begging to get inside.

The traveler, her lover, wrenched Lira up then (oh, she knew, she knew, what she wanted from the selkie, what she was compelled to give) and when their mouths touched the traveler whispered something,

something so low, Lira perhaps wasn't meant or didn't care to hear it. Perhaps it was her true name. Perhaps it was a spell.

The traveler's tongue and teeth and all the red inside her mouth felt beautiful and calm. Like floating on placid seas. She'll admit, when pressed, it was a bit heady. Not that Lira was lost for a moment, or not as lost as the traveler was. Does she remember? They slid together on the floor, the hard dusty floor, heavy against one another, their sweat thick as the skin that seemed to encompass us both, our lust so large it was hard to tell where it began and we ended.

THE CHILD OF
MIDWINTER EVE

The ground was cold and hard and the tall, thin trees pricked the sky with long, grey fingertips. It was midwinter's eve, the night before the coldest, longest, darkest day of the year—the day that would let no light into the sky, pinching closed the twinkling mouths of the stars and snuffing out the reflection of the moon. It was a time for spells, not incantations inviting love or kindness, but vengeful cries calling forth the cold to creep into the lungs, starvation to throttle the stomach, and frost to choke the throat. It was a time when only death could be called.

The folk of the wood had offered blood sacrifices to her for centuries, but in recent years the fires of the revolution left even blood scarce, and few rituals were held. Those who did make it to the wood were deserters, running from the gut-stabbing fear of the White Army or the Red. They would eventually be cut down anyway, of course, though never like they imagined. Others sought asylum, thought to make a small wood-hut and live on bark soup or else make their way to Manchuria, Turkey, America. It did not take them long to discover how difficult it was to survive in the dark land, never mind make it through it. Few made it out. And now, few ventured to the wood anymore.

On this midwinter's eve, the couple that tiptoed among the bonesplinter bushes were so gaunt they looked almost like ghosts. Yet they had feet and their eyes were not white but black and hungry.

The child poked her nose between the lower white arms of the trees and watched the couple. As they circled the clearing the child licked the sharp needles that grew from her gums. She had been waiting a long time, and though she did not need to eat as frequently as humans did, even she was hungry.

"What are we even doing here, Yuki?" The tall one had a pink mouth that was turning blue in the night air. His skin was red where the frost bit, its teeth chewing his cheeks until they were angry.

The smaller one, the woman, had eyes that shone like bitten plums: bruise-purpled skin ringing the red edges of bloodshot eyes. This terrible wetness hung in contrast to lips, torn and bloodied from biting back sobs that had dried in the freezing cold, cheeks fixed, perfect pale stones, as though no emotion could tremble through them. She was colder than the long, dark night that approached. A white scarf was braided around her neck.

"I'm doing what must be done." She stared at the man until he looked down. Then she knelt on the black ground and dug, dug until her fingernails were torn. Though the child knew it was too cold for what she craved, that sweet brown-red, to run far from any but a grievous wound, she felt her mouth water, wetting the back of her cold lips.

"What good does it do to dig holes in the woods?" the tall man murmured, eyes on the black earth. When the woman did not answer, the tall man's voice turned cold, ice and steel: "I regret lying with Onna. I regret getting her with child while you were away spurring your precious revolution. Is that what you want me to say? Will that stop the baby from being born? Will that make your barren womb quicken?" He stopped suddenly, biting his lips enough to turn them white as the snow that would soon blanket the floor of the wood.

The child wondered whether his marrow tasted of salt or sweet.

The woman did not stop digging. "Hand me the stones."

The tall man sighed and started to empty his pockets, tossing perfectly round stones to the ground. The woman took and placed them, one by one, in the hole: larger stones for the torso and legs, a smaller ring of rocks curving around the chest like tiny arms encircling growing lungs, and taken from her own pocket, a perfectly round moonstone for the head. When the snow fell from the sky it would make a cold, white shroud for this very small stone baby.

"Get me a needle from the bonesplinter bush and be quick about it."

The child leaned closer now, half her sharp face cutting out from behind the tree. She wondered if the man would be able to break the nettle from the bush without impaling himself on the thousand other barbs. The sap of the needle was filled with a poison that turned the body cold and heavy, like a cloud laden with rain. She imagined lapping the blood from each puncture in the man's skin as he lay on the hard ground in the dark. But the man leaned into the bonesplinter bush and managed to pick a needle without pricking himself. Still, the child held her breath.

"I still don't understand why I must be here," the tall man handed the sharp nettle to the small woman, who kneeled over the stone baby she had made in the ground. "This is nonsense. Do you think a silly spell will stop what already comes?"

By this time the child was digging her needle-nails into the bark of the tree to keep from betraying herself. She could smell the marrow beneath the skin now, she was sure. She wished the tall man would come closer so she could slit his belly open and lick the sweaty juices from his liver. But the woman was moving toward the man, leaning in and whispering in his ear in a quiet, dead voice that made the child become as still as fallen snow.

"Most magic that women do can be done alone. My mother built children made of snow in these woods and soon after had a child for each cold likeness she created. But this ..." the small woman gestured to the small white body in the ground, "is best done with two. Death is always better done with the blood of the one who first helped the child to life."

With a deep grunt, the small woman drove the sharp nettle into the hollow of the tall man's throat. At the force of her thrust, he fell back into the bonesplinter bush. His scream was silent, his mouth gaping, and though he struggled he could not disentangle himself from the needles. The woman turned and looked into the copse of tall thin trees.

"You will have a child," the woman said. "Just not the one you thought to have. Will she comfort you in the dark, I wonder? Or will your bones even make it into the ground?"

The man had no answer, of course.

"You may come out now." The woman's voice was strong and clear. She did not look at the man until she saw the child scurry from behind the trees to the prickly bonesplinter bush.

The child could hold herself back no more. It had been so long since she had eaten. The child of midwinter opened her mouth and the long teeth that hid behind her blue lips tore into the man's leg. His bones, though strong, broke easily for her. As she feasted, the woman unwrapped the snow white scarf that braided her own throat and dropped it into the pool of blood that was already freezing below the bush. Once the scarf was red, she laid it over the stony baby that slept in the black ground. The child would see the babe and smell the blood that soon, and not far away, would be born. And then the child would finish the job.

For now, the darkness had come. Midwinter's eve tipped over the black side of the moon to midwinter. The child feasted. The marrow of the man was sweet and soon she would wish for more.

THE BODY MAN'S MARK

It has always been his favorite spot: the hollow below the ear. He'd taken to noticing its beauty carefully in his apprentice days, without raising suspicion. He was cautious in all things; though theirs was a society obsessed with death, one could still say that one should shrink from the body men—those who prepared the dead for the next life. He saw the words "undignified" and "morbid" and "queer" float from the mouths of those who would do well to remember that death came for all. Still, he understood. His work was of the body, the flesh, every inch that was covered in life was bared to him. That had to unnerve. So he was careful, quiet, a black cat blinking yellow eyes on the top of a fence post. Barely noticed by most. But that hollow, that hollow. It made him tilt his head and close his eyes and dream things he knew he shouldn't.

∾

Do body men take wives? It had been a question that floated in his brain. Most body men he'd known before were certainly family men, cabinet makers who specialized, passing knowledge down to sons and nephews, as if any normal trade. And perhaps it was normal, the most common of all. Yet he found poor dead creatures flung at him in the village streets, ravaged corpses of birds and once, a fox, not quite dead, on the doorstep. There was so much needless anger at death, he'd thought, taking up a needle and black thread and stitching up the russet and cream collared creature. Do the bodies rage when their time is over, when it is time to become something else? Certainly they did not. He did not believe in a spirit that survived from body to body, he didn't think, but then again, as the fox stirred and flicked its tongue out to catch his thumb, he wondered at all the things he didn't know.

The daughter was beautiful and her father was dead. This was all the body man was told. The correspondence came in a golden envelope and was written in a flourishing script, which was how he surmised that the writer must be a person of beauty. It was a strange case, being far from where he found himself, close to the sea, where many said spirits could soar upon leaving the body. The Estate was a day and a night's ride from his village. He wondered why servants would not have completed the embalming and burial, for this was the custom, he thought, among the inlanders. He remembered this from a book he once read, a historical paper, some oddity that had popped into his daily existence and just as strangely, passed away. Perhaps those servants at the estate were invalided or in some way unable to help even their master in one final task.

Once he was out from under the drear skies of his dark coach, the undertaker did not notice the gilt pillars or marbled halls, the verdant lawns and lush shrubbery of the Estate. These details escaped both his attention and his imaginings. He noticed only the way the daughter did not flinch from him, offered him tea the color of the hair that hung heavy behind her ears, looked into his eyes and did not blink. Crape hung from every surface, swooned in the draughty room, billows of decay blooming through doors.

"Sir must be wanting to get on with his business." In the shadows, the maid interrupted, mouth knifing sallow cheeks.

"Yes, I suppose I must. I admit, I'm quite … surprised to be called so far inland. Was there no one to care for your father's final wishes?" He'd learned not to say words like: body, burial, coffin, death.

The daughter pressed a cup and saucer to his cold hands.

"My father was unwell these late years. He did not wish to put upon his neighbors or loved ones, and we, though we could not ease his pain, would not abandon him. I was told of you." She held the body man's eyes once more. "I trust you'll find everything you need." Her cream and rose skin paled as she slid from the room, the voluminous folds of her tawny gown trailing behind her. The movement recalled light, full movements of a creature in the dusk slipping just away from sight, movements that caught him, over and over, in waking and in dreams.

"Where shall I begin?" The body man turned to the sour face of the maid.

The maid did not answer, brought him to the cooling room where the old man was laid out, waited until he thanked her before leaving him to his duty. The father had been wizened by age, his muscle and skin thinning over his bones. His joints were bulbous and his eye sockets nearly cavernous, the milky pupils floating in the open bowls of his skull. He would stitch them shut along with the thin lips. He found trousers, vest, shirt, collar, all pressed. No cufflinks or rings. He would have made a private joke to himself at realizing he'd either not been trusted or beaten to the punch but rather, keeping his own head to task, dreamed of the tilt of the daughter's skull, the orbital crests, the smooth and stretch of the brow, nose, and small lips, the sharp curve of the ear, like a tiny pointed fruit, and the dark space behind and below. He imagined it full of scent, tuberose and wet grass.

~

"Please, you must eat something." Her concerned wafted at him from behind the crape, as if her voice were made of a heavy incense, sticking to his clothes and skin.

"Thank you, but ..." It wasn't that he was quite unaccustomed to kindness; he was quite unaccustomed to being noticed, particularly on a job.

That was all he remembered, all there was of their conversation, really. He could spin it round and round like a carousel horse and grow a yarn long enough to string all the lights of the stars but what would that be to him but a torture? He did not look longingly and she did not lean ever so slightly, her chin pressing the heavily perfumed air before her, exposing the beautiful, dark hollow where her skull and neck met.

~

The fox had been acting rather strangely, he supposed, though he had little experience with them. Once, as a boy, he had found a nest of kits and brought them into the house. His mother had started sliding the slope of her nervous disease, after his brother, William, had been still-born, and every one of the household taken by the influenza. She had screamed and cuffed his ears, not realizing that her heavy rings could graze, slice the side of his face, his ear, his neck.

"How could you do this? How could you?"

He had imagined his mother cuddling the soft tawny fluff beneath her neck, cupping her palm to his cheek and kissing him, like she did before William. Instead she ordered him to return them to their nest immediately. He had told her that he would do whatever she wanted. Whatever she needed to make her better. He'd stopper his tears. He'd do it for her. Even when he heard the kits crying in the night, their mother long gone.

This creature was grown and wary of humans, though it let him scratch its ear and nudged his hand when it decided it was hungry. It was mostly content to ignore him unless it had a need. None of the other villagers seemed to notice or bother with it, though they often turned their noses up at the queer smells the creature brought with it. One morning, after spending all night refitting a coffin for the florid publican, the fox leaned into his trousers, wetting them with a blanket of cold dew. The icy wetness jolted him away from his task, which was nearly done, and alerted him to a pot a tea and plate of rashers that had been deposited for him while he was deep in work. He didn't trouble himself to think of who had concerned themselves but threw a rasher to the fox who made short work of it, and set into his portion, both tearing through the meat savagely.

In the night, the fox ran through his dreams, led him through thickets until its paws were bloody and its body was thick with sweat.

He could never catch it. Upon waking the fox would be at his bedside, pressing wet paws to his brow, wide eyes watching for his breath.

～

He was surprised to be called back to the Estate, so soon after the father's death. Was there a dispute over payment? Surely he wouldn't be called directly for that, nor would his services be required for a gardener or house servant. The hansom drove through the gloom and his heart pumped more blood than his body had a right to have.

The estate was mostly dark. A servant dressed in crape brought him up the front stair rather than through to the drawing room, which was most unorthodox. One was rarely permitted into the boudoir unless it was unavoidable.

The anteroom was full of roses, silk, damask, perfumed.

He finally understood.

"Where is she?"

The maid, whose face was now hidden behind a floor-length veil that obscured not just her face, but her entire form, said nothing. She swept her hand to the left and a gilt and sky door pushed back, revealing a dark gap in the fabric of the wall.

He stepped quiet, sure of what was on the other side. Don't hesitate, he ordered himself. Do it for her.

Her eyes were open, her gaze bent to the door as if she had been waiting for him, which he knew was ridiculous. Someone had tucked her up as if she were only sleeping, and tried to slip roses under her hands, which bore the blood of the thorns and had stained the counterpane. It didn't matter now, did it? He knew that he should be getting to work, time still ticks for the living when it comes to fresh corpses, but something made him stop. Kneeling in a pool of black lace, he leaned into her. He might have thought it an oddity for someone so young to have so many meters of black lace in her boudoir but perhaps he would have thought it relic of her father's recent death. Really, he didn't think of anything at all, except the soft curve of her chin beneath his hands, his fingers dipping into the shadows that pooled below her ear, that darkness that he dove into, that enveloped him, that would never release him.

In sleep, the fox nudged his shoulder, curled beneath his master's breast and slept.

THE PAINTER

She never knew what was going to happen until she started stabbing her palette knife into the canvas. Never knew what stories the pigment was going tell, whether it would whisper or scream as it flowed out on the gessoed cotton duck. She was only the medium.

The stories usually started like this: thick and dark, full of pleas and woe, of have-nots and now never-woulds. Most of the time, the thick coagulations would spread out under her knife, become thin and confess to crimes, perhaps hoping for mercy, though where they thought that would come from she didn't know.

The first time she realized that human pigment was alive, it wasn't a revelation. She can't recall whether it was at the hands of this lover or that stranger; she'd bled so much back then. She only remembers lying with her face against the paneling of her trailer (or maybe it was in that office), thick fluid from her split jaw seeping, smearing the wood each time she moaned until a sideways mouth arced on the wall. And then the mouth started to scream. It started to tell her all the things, all the true things, things she needed to hear: *You are alive. You are breathing. You are not beaten.* She wanted the voice to keep talking. To keep telling her what to do. And it did.

She soon found out that there are many voices in human pigment. So many stories and pleas and she wanted to hear them all, had to hear them all, commit them to canvas, show the world who everyone really was, the things that they did. For when you spread the red around, painted with it, it confessed, it comforted. It told her she'd done right.

Tonight's story is nothing like the others: it is screamed by countless voices that lick her ears with their torment until she feels her skin will melt, until she feels that they are inside her, manipulating her instead of she manipulating them. The stories aren't confessions but tales of terrible death at the hands, the mouth of the creature she's stabbed in the jugular, the creature that lies in the bathtub behind her. The stories gush at her, biting her face and mouth, and she can't translate their despair fast enough, the canvas won't hold them all, and as she turns, she sees that the pigment continues to pour from the monster (oh, she is sure he is a monster, more monster than she) and she knows now that they will not stop until she has carried them all inside her, told them all. She cannot run from the stories; they know she is there. Even after the room and the motel walls are red, even after the police come and slip the crisp white jacket over her arms, even after she is showered and locked up and dull with drugs, they will stay with her, consuming the only comfort she had ever known.

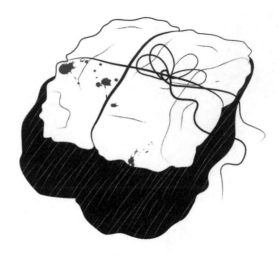

OUR COURTSHIP, OUR ROMANCE

Their bodies are beautiful. All moonstone pale, necklaced and braceleted with rubies, rubies dripping down their naked flesh. I always undress them, knowing he grows impatient with bustles and corsets, and those horrid gloves. The things girls are taught will win them husbands. Before he found me, he'd never yet met a woman that wasn't fond of these insipid enclosures. He'd ripped miles of cloth from trembling arms, long as swans' necks and just as indignant. Perhaps this is what draws him to me. Nothing pleases me like tearing boundaries, breaking bindings said to be unbreakable.

It had been stormy that night, and all of town was tittering. There was a new suitor at the big house, a bearded gentleman, horrid and French. Rumors followed him. They said he took his wives away to a castle by a distant ocean, and they were never heard from again. They said he was a monster, that he slit their throats when they displeased him and fucked them while they were dying. Of course, they said similar things about me. That I fucked my father, that I killed him when I could no longer take the betrayal in my mother's eyes. That I killed them both. They also said that the darkest souls would search for a darker match, that they'd commit murder, heresy, until they found it. Rumors can be just as sharp as knives.

I love to decorate my chamber with their flesh, their sighs, their screams. Draping one across a settee and softly pressing her breasts to mine; pounding another into the pianoforte, my thrusts fisting her spine into the stained ivory; and then the quick slap of a blushing face peeking out from behind the velvet portières. They are lovely, and they are mine.

Not bothering to shield himself from the rain pouring from the sky, the servant boy had scurried across the back doorstep, panting hot clouds—orders from the suitor. He wished to see me in his quarters.

"A present for his new mistress? Perhaps a pork roast to celebrate the impending nuptials?" I asked. The boy did not answer, but hiccoughed, trembling breath into the night air. I leaned close and whispered, "How did he hear of my talents with the knife?"

The boy said nothing. He was afraid. They all were, enough to have kept me around. I've often wondered why, in those days of fear and inquisition, I had not been strung up for a witch. Was it that no one could cleave meat from bone as quickly as I could? Perhaps it was simply a paralyzing combination of disgust and fear. The dead butcher's daughter and likely his killer, carver of bloody flesh who carries the stench of death even in her Sunday finery.

"I will come when I am ready," I told the boy. "Tell your master that."

I prepared his gift, stripped down to my skin as I drove the cleaver, separated flesh from bone, heart from chest. I wondered how he would receive it. If he would prove worthy. As I worked, I thought of the girl in the big house, anticipating her betrothal, of girls in fairy tales, white and simpering and virginal before their suitors: dark huntsman and princes. They knew nothing of men, really. Nothing of dark desires. How there's nothing you can do but give in to them.

My husband, well, he rarely pleasures himself with them. I believe he finds that he'd much rather watch me make them pant, swear, and beg before I spend their blood upon the stone floor. And when I grow tired of their bodies, when their faces become too silly and stiff for my liking, they go into his chamber, a dank and depressing place in the bowels of the castle, locked behind a door that no one, not even I, can break down.

Like Cleopatra and the carpet, I wound my blood-smeared body in butcher paper and twine. I stuck my longest, sharpest knife between my breasts and, seeing the rain had stopped, carried my gift through the cold night air to the big house. Clutching the offering, I walked alone, the servant long since having skittered away. I remember seeing visions in my mind: long, pale hands slowly ripping yards of opal cloth away from trembling arms and the sticky slick that the carving knife leaves behind. The hands were mine and yet they were not mine. They floated and clasped and wrung themselves in ecstasy and terror. Girls are as dark as shadows and just as clever, as I was then. Barely more than a girl, yet I knew what I wanted: a lover, a partner, an equal.

He found me at his door, stared into me with endless sea-glass eyes, took the end of the twine that bound the rough paper to my flesh between his fingertips, and pulled me into his room. When I was beyond the threshold, I held out his gift: the largest pig's heart from my stores, trussed in a lace garter and stuffed with a perfect, blood-soaked apple. He stood so still, my string wrapped around the small column of his finger. One pull and I would have been in his arms, at his mercy, perhaps. Instead, I held his eyes, slid the long knife out of its hiding place between my breasts and slipped it through the rough skin of the pig heart. I held out a slice of the dripping morsel on the point of the blade and pressed it to his pale lips.

He collects them for me. Travels far and wide and finds the perfect girls. Delectable girls. Once, he even found a girl with paintings inked into her skin, covering every inch of her. She said they were stories from her homeland. In the end, she was no sweeter, had no more tales to tell, than all the others.

When I grow tired of a certain girl, he procures another, telling her that she'll be his wife, have all that she desires, if only she will come away to his large castle, submit to his dark and forbidding nature, reign as queen over everything, except, of course, the tallest tower chamber and the deepest, darkest room. Give a woman a key and tell her no. She'll take everything. She'll want what's behind the door even more than her own life. How breathtaking it is to see—a woman, who really is many women, searching just outside darkness's door, yet most can never quite push through, can never quite find the power there.

The transformation of his face in that moment is tattooed on my memory. His mouth was red with blood, his eyes floated back in his head and I felt the groan that escaped his throat deep within my cunt. I could smell the salt that beaded at his brow. It reminded me of the scent of pigs rutting in mud, full of desperation, the pulse of animal need. I fed him the heart in my hands, piece by piece, and my desire dripped down my legs, pooling with the blood on the Persian carpet. When the heart was gone, he knelt at my feet, sweat dripping into the pool of blood and come. His grey-green eyes held mine, and, again, beautiful visions of torture, of lust, floated in my mind: shackles embracing writhing wrists, mouths with dagger tongues piercing flesh, fingertips squeezing nipples blue with lack of blood. I wanted them all. I wanted him to give them to me.

I didn't have to tell him what to do next: he already knew what I needed, dragging his fingers through the sticky pool where our desires comingled. His breath was a gift, a benediction on my thigh, as he leaned forward and, after kissing the knife with which I fed him the heart, slid it out of my hand. Dipping the already wet steel in the pool between us, he brushed the blade up the sturdy bones of my ankle, colored the crescent of my calf. (How long since I had stood slaughtering pigs? Forever, it seemed.) As the mixture of our lust spread on my skin, the blade grew dry. Again, he slowly, slowly brought the knife to the pool and languidly swirled the steel, taking care to wet the entire length of the blade. I lost control then, panting like an animal just as it knows death is coming, just as it spills its seed.

He gave me a soft smirk.

"Please ... ," I breathed. In all my life, it was the only time I have ever begged.

Slower than the sweetest slaughter, he undid me. His breath hot and wet on my skin, never far behind the blade. He slid the red knife up my thigh, parted my butcher paper dress, and, upon reaching my sex, spread me open and pressed the heavy handle of the knife to my clit. With the knife between our bodies, I fell into him, hands tangling in his midnight-blue hair, and gave him the first of many orders: "Harder."

He obliged me with a sigh, like a suckling pig at its mother's teat.

I traced his face with my palms, wanting more from him, needing him inside my flesh.

I took the blade in my hand and ground it into my clit, and he—a clever, knowing man—drove the pointed dagger of his tongue into my cunt over and over, until all that existed were the parts of us that promised pleasure and pain, the parts of us that made sense.

Later, when he cut my butcher paper dress away and painted the rest of my body with his mouth, cutting with the blade, soothing with his tongue, he made the darkness that floated in my soul feel right, free, like it belonged there. Like I needed it and he needed me.

Together, we become perfect, our flawed bodies pressing and writhing on cold stones. The blood, the knives, the screams—everything that we do and that we are floats away, halos spinning like last breaths around our heads. The only thing remaining in the world is us, together. Our flesh answering our flesh, our souls no longer seeking. We are the boundaries that we break. We are love.

TRANSFORMATIONS

Every time you do it, you try to remember that once it disgusted you, that you schemed and cried to keep away from this threshold, this room of death. But it doesn't matter if it once made you sick and sorry, there is no repenting now. You do what you have to do.

Remember that first time, how you bent back the iron nails holding the skin in place, the skin you herbed, oiled, loved. Then, you'd slid that piece of hide (supple with spells, her spells, but mostly yours now) from the birch wood stretcher, still red with her blood, and laid it on the butcher block, the place where she'd made your meals and you fucked that first time and many after, her inside you, before you even knew that's what you wanted. Force yourself to recall the feel of her teeth and nails and then her tongue, running down down down your neck as you caressed that last piece of her with the sharp blade, outlined the ruddy bird whose wings once beat against her chest, before you cut it away as she died. Held her final screams and her blanking eyes in your mouth and swallowed them as you sliced the tattooed skin into three strips, hoping they'd be easier to sew into who you had become, easier to choke down.

~

"Where will you be, if you're not in this world or the next? The waiting room? The drive through of the Taco fucking Bell?" You threw the nearest book across the floor toward her. Not that you'd ever deliberately tried to hit her. You couldn't do anything to hurt anyone, not then; you couldn't even get her stupid cats, who scrambled across the room at your fitful display, to leave your plants alone. It was Cynthia, beautiful Cynthia who had all the power, who soaked up the electricity in a room until it crackled from her fingertips.

"It's not like that. You know it." The wind slapped the storm windows and Cynthia's voice rose with it. You hated storms, darkness, anger. You hated the flavor that darkness left on your tongue, even as your lover seemed to thrive on it. Not that Cynthia was half as bitter that day as she'd been when you first knew her. The cancer had taken so much of her fire away.

You closed your eyes. It was all too loud in your brain, like every thought and fear that you'd been trying to keep out since you knew Cynthia was dying had slid in through your ears and spread into all of the secret corners, the ones you kept even from her. You wondered what death would be like if the ritual worked: the pulsing darkness of a new mind, the sounds of the living word amplified, bouncing through a skull that wasn't really hers, no longer able to control what happened to her. It seems silly, thinking about it now, after everything, that Cynthia would ever have let herself be out of control. Especially in death.

"All matter is made up of the same material ..." She began her lecture, the one that her students had always loved, the one you'd come to both dread and cherish; the possibilities it contained: all matter being the same, and when matter dies it does not cease to exist but transforms, becomes ... something else. Heavier pieces of air and cloud and star that travel and exist beyond our physical plane, our visual plane.

"But if transmogrification rites are performed at the moment of death, there is a possibility that the spirit will be weighted down, that the energy released at the moment of physical death will not be released but instead contained, at least for a time, and if, of course, there is a vessel to hold it." You finished for her. It's what she wanted from you, wasn't it? No matter how afraid you were of what happened next. No matter how ill-prepared you were to do what needed to be done.

Cynthia opened her eyes, stared into you until you sank down into the middle of the carpet, the seed, the tiny pod of possibility that you could have ever backed out closed in your fist. Even in sickness you could never have disobeyed her.

"But what if I can't do it? What if ..." You wanted to ask: who's going to protect me? Does anyone care who I will become?

"I'm dying. There is only one way we can get to the other side of this. And it's together."

You knew it was a lie. But you loved her enough to pretend to believe you couldn't live without her, that what you'd both become once on the other side would be recognizable.

~

The thing about energy is that it isn't tame. Especially spirit energy. And containing it is akin to trying to trap an open flame in a box of splintered wood: even if it works for a time, the container is volatile, and in the end the only way for the spirit to live again is for it to be consumed whole. For one fire to devour another.

You don't understand this, not at first—that transformation means sacrifice. Nor did you grasp the gravity of what Cynthia had asked you to do, the dark work that had to be done, until you had to finish the ritual.

And hadn't Cynthia exhausted all other options before she asked this of you? Sometimes, even now, you feel her whispering to you in the night, a hot breath on your thigh, making you believe, accept: she'd done everything she could—prepared the room, gathered the oils, the fenugreek, the pot of basil, the other, sweeter spices. She'd even carved the drying board from the heart of an ancient beech tree, bent iron nails around the edges and painted it blood red.

By the time she was ready, Cynthia had lost her hair, the blond tresses with the roots as dark as grave dirt. Her fingernails and toenails and nearly all of her body fat (and some of her organs) had been eaten away by the cancer and her flesh was as thin as onion skins. Her tattoo, a ruby-throated hummingbird that floated between her clavicle and her breasts was the only burst of color, of life, left on her body. God, how you loved fluttering your fingers over her skin, mimicking the beating of wings as you lay behind her, holding her thinning body, stroking the wings as she shivered over and over and over, never warm again.

"The fenugreek, the oils, the spices..."

"All in the spice closet." You finished, eyes on the pot of basil that sat by the head of the bed, your fingers twining in their green stalks like they once caught in the tendrils of Cynthia's hair. Don't think about her hair, you warned yourself. You'll never be able to do this if you think about her hair.

"Every night. And during the day ..." Cynthia began, but a coughing fit left her breathless, and you dropped to your knees, submerged a tiny, pink sponge in a bowl of distilled water, and swabbed the inside of Cynthia's cheeks, her tongue, until her mouth was moist. You lied to yourself: told yourself that you'd soothed her, soothed her throat as much as it could be in her final moments in this body.

"I know. Nested in basil and watered with brine. At least until ..."

Cynthia's raw coughs wracked her thinned body once more and she pled:

"Please, Al, please. Do it now."

Trembling, you took the bone knife in your left hand, pressed your right palm into the paper-thin skin of Cynthia's chest and held her down. Cynthia couldn't fight—there was nothing left but the weak thumps of her failing heart beating its last against your sweaty palm, the shaking of your own fingers frantic and grasping, unable to catch hold of the flickering rhythms. Tears dripped down your face and mixed with blood as you began to trace the knife lightly around the edges of the humming-bird tattoo. It didn't matter that you had to stop three times to vomit on the carpet, that you shook until the wings of the bird were feathered with blood; the blade itself was keen enough that you didn't have to sharpen it to continue, not once. You thought about slitting your wrists and letting the hospice nurse find both of your bodies, but you could not stop feeling the tiny pulses of life in Cynthia's skin. Even after Cynthia had closed her eyes for the last time, and the tattoo was stretched and oiled and herbed and nestled in the pot of basil, watered with your own tears, you felt the beating of the tiny wings against your palms.

∾

Days passed before you could even leave the house—you were afraid that something would happen to the skin when you left. You were caught in the doorway between nightmares, unable to look at what was behind you, even as you felt the breath of the past on your neck. Your slick palm pressed on the door to what awaited you. Surely, you would be swallowed by the new darkness behind it. All of the cats had shunned you, acting more aloof than was usual, even for creatures who had never preferred you to begin with. No matter where you put the basil pot, they always seemed to find it, marking their territory around the base of the planter and sometimes even chewing the leaves, as if they knew you were doing something wrong, something you shouldn't do. Yet the basil continued to grow, the clean scent of the leaves hiding the spicy odor of the preserved skin lying beneath the green tendrils.

"I miss you, I need you, I can't do this without you," you whispered to the pot, hoping it would answer. You hadn't learned to be angry. Not yet.

Every morning and every night, you removed the skin from the green depths of the pot. It took you weeks to be able to do this without sobbing; when you touched the skin, you felt the knife in your hands, your lover's life draining out beneath your wet fingers all over again. But some whisper, its voice a fluttering beat, kept telling you that it didn't matter what it did to you: the tattooed skin had to be kept supple and alive at all costs.

And what about me? You asked the voice, fingers pressing into the greasy layers of red epidermis over and over and over. And always, the answer: "On your own? You're nothing without love."

So you kept tending the pot, oiling the skin, knowing the moment would come soon where the doors to the past, the present, would close.

～

Those early days were difficult, and when you thought you'd finally made the decision to leave, when you began packing your trunk, selling your books, leaving the white beechwood out on the table overnight with a hammer beside it, locking the cats in the garden, Cynthia would come to you in your dreams. She looked different each time. She was still Cynthia, of course, but she was Cynthia when she was in her early twenties, before you'd met, or Cynthia as a rough teen, studs in her nose, long, Stevie Nicks hair tucked into a glittery scarf. Once she'd even come to you as a child, a small thing with ripped cut-offs and bloody knees. Child Cynthia wanted to be held. And so you held her: curled around her tiny, pale body, and wrapped your arms around this girl, who said her name was Cindy, and held her tight until she fell asleep. She was gone, of course, when the sun made its way through the cracks in the blinds, and it was then that the loss of Cynthia, of your Cynthia, of all the Cynthias became real again, made you sure that getting Cynthia back was as urgent as the blood pumping in your fingers, in her little piece of skin, and keeping her alive, whatever the cost to your mind, your soul, didn't matter.

After that the best dreams would come to you. Cynthia was invisible, but you could feel her tongue curling around the place where your ear met your throat, following your breath along your neck to the dip in to your clavicle, the smooth, teasing path down your chest, all the way down below the curve of your belly. And always then, the too-light touch of fingertips pressing gently into your thighs, her thumbs sweeping the sensitive skin before too many moments passed, and then a laugh and Cynthia's mantric whisper: "Patience ..."

Exasperation met ecstasy when Cynthia's tongue licked you open, pushed into you, deeper and deeper, until your whole body was burning with electricity, with cold, with two bodies now becoming one, spirit and flesh alike, until you woke, crying out with your climax, alone in the bed but for the promise of transformation, of what you would be when you were together again, forever this time.

~

A month after Cynthia's death, she'd really started haunting you, though perhaps you were always haunted, even from the beginning. Cynthia came to you, but not as she had ever been in life, of that you felt certain. She was colorless. Her body shifted from a block of grey to blue-black and back again. Her features would shift, lose definition, become subsumed in the static cloud of her body.

Sometimes she was a corpse. You cannot, will not, recall those dreams. Only that they drove you, vomiting, to the loo, where you'd spend the night, curled on the bath rug, surrounded by some of the older cats, the grey one and the white one, Fish and Pearl. They'd been the first to shun you after Cynthia left, the first to hiss and bite as you swatted them away from the pot of basil, though now they seemed to take pity on you, sometimes, even to love you.

The bathroom tile was cool on your cheek and you'd almost slipped into dream when a clammy palm wound around your neck, soft blond curls brushed your cheek and lips supple with spiced oil whispered:

"I'm here, darling. I can tell you everything you need to do. I can stop the pain. Only, you must listen to me. Do everything I say."

∼

The weeks went on, and you tried to be so good. Your sobs stopped at the bottom of your throat. You fed the cats, even as they spat at you, and oiled the skin and told yourself that Cynthia really could feel each stroke. Sometimes you even felt the wings of the hummingbird beat a soft, coy flutter against your fingers. With each flit, a part of you flaked away, like dead skin. You were becoming hard and powerful and you could do anything, couldn't you? You could bring her back.

You poured oil on your fingers and with one hand, retraced the paths of Cynthia's ghost tongue, circling and pulling and pressing into your body while your other hand was buried deep in the basil pot, copying each urgent ministration on the supple and stretched hummingbird tattoo. You brought yourself off again and again and each time you could feel your jaw set and spine straighten and muscles tighten and you knew. You knew your strength for the first time. You knew you could complete the ritual.

∼

In your final dream of her, Cynthia was just as she was before she died. Early 30s, wearing her tarot card earrings, and nothing else. She was lying right next to you, but you couldn't feel Cynthia's body at all; in place of her touch, you felt the cold of metal or something like it.

She said nothing, only looked in your eyes, as her cats, all of them now, curled around you on the bed. A physics book lay open on your belly, notes scribbled in the margins. Some of the handwriting Cynthia's, some of it yours. You'd been interested in matter lately, all the theories of matter that you'd never had the head for before, suddenly it was all you could think about.

"It's time, Cynthia." You stroked Pearl's head, her snaggletooth lovingly biting the meat of your slick palm.

Cynthia had told you all about the final aspect of the ritual before she died. It was the part that you'd dreaded the most. Transferring the spirit from the skin to its permanent vessel. In that moment, though, you weren't so afraid. You had begun to understand strength, had come to know the steel in your own bones. And even then, even as you were in bed with a ghost, even as Cynthia opened her mouth and screamed silently—her tarot card earrings flickering, The Tower and The Star flashing instead of what you know the cards should be (you had them in her dresser drawer for fuck's sake): The Empress and The Lovers—you didn't close your eyes. You stared into the eyes of the ghost until she could only fade, her earrings, dark nipples, the dip of her belly, constellations slowly burning out into the nothing of the night air in the bedroom.

Then you gently scooped the skin from beneath the basil. You licked it, tasted the sensual power in the oily magic, washed your body with its spells. Every time it caressed you, you wondered how you'd lived so much of your life without knowing how good strength felt, how strong the skin of your lover made you, and how you could keep that feeling forever.

∿

His hands are on you before you can even lead him to the room you've prepared: sliding down your shoulders, grabbing at the leather that covers your chest. Your laugh feels strange in your throat—whose idea had the outfit been? Cynthia's, of course. She'd always been the daring adventurous one, the smart one. It had been easy to make the plan once Cynthia's voice fluttered against your skin, whispered exactly what was needed.

"What are you laughing at?" The man's eyes are dulled with drink, his hands calloused from carrying two by fours or driving rigs or whatever he said he did before he stuck his tongue in your ear at the dark end of the bar. Not that it will matter tomorrow. None of that will matter tomorrow. At least not for him.

"I'm not laughing ..." You look into his eyes. You used to look away from questions, soft glances, you used to close your eyes and deny your strength, hide within the shell of yourself.

He pushes you into an old vanity. The sharp metal of your belt clanks on the glass top.

"No laughing."

He's distracted with scolding you, with drink, with his hardness pressing into you through your clothes, and he never even feels the tip of the blade as it presses into the crook of his arm.

"You're going to help me," you whisper, touch your tongue lightly to his upper lip as you lean in. He wants to say yes. Everyone is hungry for something. Especially you.

He doesn't even swear, doesn't even jump as the lip of the blade opens his clothes, his skin. Most of the vessels protest, at least a bit, at least at first. He just lies there, red ribboning down his arm, puddling beneath him on the bed. Perhaps he thinks this a game.

You cup the blood in your palms: it's a thick syrup, not the bright red of poison apples, the imagined dangers of the life you used to lead, but the rust of old wire, that which binds the flesh, makes it burst and bleed. You drip it carefully on his neck, his chest, down his calves and arms, saturate the dark hair between his legs.

You wonder what his skin will look like flecked with blood and seed and sweat. Will they look like all the others?

Slowly, you unpick the buttons of the leather vest. Do you remember when you used to flinch away from death? Cry and tear your hair? You lean down and dip a finger into the deepening pool beneath his shoulder, run your fingers across your chest. You turn to the pot of basil, and so gently lift the skin from beneath the thick tendrils.

He trembles and lets a gasp escape his paling lips and you know that he's almost ready.

Carefully, so carefully, you place the skin on his chest. He's lost so much blood, but he's still breathing. The hummingbird flutters and you can't tell where his skin ends and Cynthia's begins. You miss her so much. You always will. You push your jeans down your legs, your skin already fragrant with basil, fenugreek. He watches you, and as you climb atop him you see that he is afraid, like Cynthia was afraid, all those years ago. You are stronger than even Cynthia thought you were. When it's covered in fresh blood, the blood of the dying, the little square of what's left of her thrums and beats and whispers to you, shares secrets and spells and pleases you with stories, with love and promises and togetherness, for surely part of your strength is that you are never, ever alone. Cynthia told you with her dying breaths that this would work and she was right. She was right, though no one has been able to replace her, not really.

~

Afterwards you wash the skin. The blood nourishes it and it is pink for weeks after even with oiling. You tend to it as a lover would; you keep the house and the plants. You feed the cats. Some nights you wake up and can't remember who you are, where you are. The skin stays moist in the pot of basil and the tendrils grow thick and gnarled and long; they cover windows and they cover doors, soaking the light and the air until you feel you can breathe only in short bursts, the air pricking your lungs like hummingbird wings beating their way through your throat, through your lips, drowning in the air.

THE SCENT OF LOVE

Young men's love then lies not
truly in their hearts, but in their eyes.

— William Shakespeare

He faces her and for now the world is just them, everything quiet save for the sound her shoe makes on its trip up and down her opposite calf, tearing the already raw flesh on her leg.

"What's your name?"

She looks down, bounces her shoe on a stone, stares hard: "Elizabeth ..."

His brain registers the struggling, slothly response. Then he blinks, lets it go, drifts on to the next sensory information his brain can take in without overload. He's just woken up, after all.

"What's your name?"

She repeats the question. Her tongue is heavy with sleep, a dead weight in her mouth, pulling open her blank expression.

It smells like lilacs and something else. Sense of smell, in the wild, is often the difference between noticing the stink of a predator before it is too late and being a tasty meal. But he's new, and he can't quite put his finger on what the scent is, this strange something that won't leave his nose, his mouth. He wonders, briefly, if she smells it too.

"What's your name?"

She has been repeating the question while he was lost in his thoughts, repeating it until the hard pink muscle starts to curl beneath her broken teeth.

His name is the thing he has trouble with. He looks down at the torn flesh on her leg, notices it's not bleeding, not like he knows it should. He looks down at his own trousered legs and takes in the immaculate creases, the cleanly clipped toenails. He turns around and walks away.

~

"What's your name?"

Today, instead of shuffling off in another direction before he answers, towards something he can never seem to find, he looks over his shoulder and says: "Mahoney."

And then, after considering, a new thing his brain has learned to do, he expresses a thought: "It's safe there."

He nods towards the small, stone house that she has been looking at. It's across the way from where they are standing at the edge of the woods, its sides cloaked in lilacs and the feeling of something he doesn't recognize, something slightly wrong.

"It's my …" He's searching for the right word to convey what this place is to him. The orderly stone façade, the rows of slab, the smooth bed on which he rests. Words are like stones floating in his brain. He finally settles on: "... home."

She nods twice, her head loose and heavy as porcelain on a marionette string, and falls to the ground.

~

Everything is black. She's inside her head now and he isn't here. She starts to remember. Of course, later she won't know she remembered herself. She won't even remember the blackness, fading into something she should easily recognize.

She's sitting among the stones.

She's sitting on a wooden plank near something large and shimmery, a lake, and the sun is in her eyes, partially blinding her and partially illuminating everything. She can see round things bobbing up and down on the water, can hear screaming laughter, and she knows that they've left her, that now she's alone.

A man's angry voice cuts across her thoughts. "Beth!"

The world goes dark again.

~

"What's your name?"

She kicks the flat stone with bare toes, having lost her shoes somewhere in this sprawling garden, up the trees, among the stones and mouths the syllables slow: "Eli .. za .. bet ..."

Her speech has slowed recently, her mouth heavier now, full of the scent of lilacs, overgrown grass and something she can't quite put her finger on. Something she knows she wants.

She stares at him expectantly, waiting for what, she doesn't know, but it's important nonetheless.

"Mahoney."

He says it, gives it to her without looking behind him. Like a bread-crumb.

Searching his face for something that's been missing, she blacks out.

~

"Beth! Beth!"

They are all in the water. They are all running. They are playing a trick on her. They are afraid.

She is tired of playing this game. She has her dress and her mother's stockings and even uncomfortable dancing shoes, so important for attracting the right boy on the party boat. Isn't that what is supposed to happen? Isn't she supposed to find the prince, though she has a boy she loves?

She had promised her mother not to lose them in the woods, her family or the shoes. The shoes were precious, an heirloom spun of glass, blood, and the spit of eunuchs or some nonsense. Her mother knew how she lost things she shouldn't, how she liked to wander off. She liked to pry the bark off of trees to see what was beneath. Sometimes she found treasure—love letters and old musty ribbons. Mostly she found bugs, whole insect kingdoms. She had even taken one with her once, the queen of a colony of hundred-legged monsters. When the bug tried to suck at her skin, to bite her, she smashed it with her shoe until it was just goop.

~

She lies beside the stone, moss tickling her tummy, mushing green on top of the red that stains the skin of her abdomen, her clothes. She picks at the moss that has leeched over the corners of the marble, making it hard to decipher.

When he comes, she pretends not to notice. He is like her, but different still. She can't put her finger on it.

"What is your name?"

She picks a final bit of moss off the right edge of the stone. "B … e … t?"

Her brow furrows. There was something else but she can't remember it.

He looks at her, squinting his eyes and says, sure of himself: "Mahoney."

❧

With her head lolling in the grass, skirt rucked up around her waist, she could be in the middle of a clandestine tryst. Seeing her like this, he is finally able to know her. It took him awhile to awaken from the twilight sleep of near death, the bite that delivered it to him, that made him what he is. Now that he is awake, he knows himself, and he knows her, the way she's lying in the grass, laboring over her breath, long legs splayed out and hands clutching at earth in the last paroxysms of … what? Death? Orgasm? He should have it stored away somewhere; he recognizes the picture in front of him but can't find the particular memory strand that will lead him to the specific time, place, the answer.

And she, she is slowly losing the ability to do anything but respond to want, whether in the form of emotional or physical hunger and bodily sensation, or in the dark saturations of pleasure and pain. She is being pushed further and further into a small stone room in the center of her brain, a room that can neither retain nor receive who she was before this. Who she was sits outside of the room, surrounded by smoke, and smell, and memory.

He, on the other hand is knowing. His brain, his body, is sharpening. He is retaining the information, yet sloughing off the excess of his humanity, his person and feeling based memories merely cold slides in his head that he catalogues as he becomes calculating, efficient, sure of what he wants, who he is.

~

"How ... I"

Her mouth gapes, teeth bared, blood of her bitten tongue staining the off-white enamel a dark brown.

He knows how these teeth, that tongue, swirled his lips and once, even nipped playfully. They are pictures moving inside him, a film reel with no emotional tether, like the flipping of cards in order to match them to others in a childhood memory game, an identification with what is already in front of him.

"How ... I"

It is a growl now, more animal than human and he remembers the night he took her among these tall stones, their first time, their last. Her skirt, belled out like a flower, the air smelling of lilacs and ... their sweat, the dew of desperation, of longing, of needing something very, very badly. Something you shouldn't want to take.

He had loved her, whatever that word could mean to him now.

∾

She is all want, emotion and need, and she wants the boy. She won't ever develop the ability to stalk or trick her targets, and even if she did, they'll always know what she is about. Which is what makes this game fun.

Even her name has left her now, every part of her former self, the details of her story, her demise, is shut outside the little stone room in her head, banging to get in, never quite making it. Not without some kind of chemical help. Smell, for example, is a powerful tool, the key that can unlock almost anything you have lost in the recesses, the tight and tiny corners of your memory. A whiff of a certain perfume can awaken sensory pathways to memories that have been repressed, locked out.

This is what she doesn't remember: how her family forbade her to see the boy again, how they took her away to the lakes, how she was so angry that she did not call for help when their boat capsized, but instead ran deep into the woods until she become lost, freezing to death half inside the bark of a fallen tree where her boy somehow found her days later. Her brain had seemed all thorns and party dresses; single-minded once on target, one might say.

∾

She was beautiful.

The boy remembers her funeral. He was the only one left to mourn her. He chose the organdy dress, the one he always thought a bit pretentious, a bit silly. But she loved it. Glowed in it in fact. He hid the bite from the priest, one of the last left to perform the internment. Perhaps he was only a curate. Not that it matters now.

He curled into his own family crypt after the last bit of earth fell on her casket and imagined what it felt like to have soil falling over your head. He'd never have to know, of course. He slept then.

And when he woke, what would he be? A cold, efficient, calculating beast who can use his memories, his "living experience" without emotional attachments, to out-trick, out-maneuver whatever may come into his path? Or the brute, hungry force that can access neither memory nor emotion, that only knows the desire to feed?

And how better to see, to know, the possibility of ruthlessness than with lovers?

~

She wants him. They both know it.

They've been dancing for days. Their meetings at their respective burial places have evolved into near touches. Her expectant looks, the coming answers that used to indicate interest have subtly changed. She doesn't care for answers any longer and in truth, he doesn't need to give them any longer.

The boy knows what he must do.

It was always about survival, really. And she, beauty though she was, was only about getting her way, even if that meant not making it to the next round. She wouldn't be here without him, he thinks as he views her gore-splattered dress, remnants of squirrels, foxes, birds and other small creatures who wander unwarily into the cemetery drying on her arms, legs. It has been awhile since she has fed.

Too bad she'll never get that big kill, feel the tongue-popping delight of grey matter bubbling with blood in her mouth. Too bad he'll have to take her for his own.

He's known it for a while now. Even found a bowie knife stuck in a large vase inside his mausoleum. He was sure it hadn't been there before. He wonders if he left it there, before. It's the only thing he doesn't remember from when he was alive, human.

∾

He leans in to her, teasing. He is coquettish, like she was.

She can smell his sweat but not her own. She is calm and if her heart beat, it would do so like an old grandfather clock, tick, tock, keeping time with the long swing of the pendulum.

He is holding something and for a minute she is catapulted back to a memory, one that has been breathing its last outside the tiny stone room in her diminished brain. She, he, here. Nighttime. Flowers. He inside her. Death.

She leans into the thing in his hand and just as he is turning to show her something else, she inhales the purple thing he is holding. And it is this nasal intoxication that makes the already loose walls of the stone room begin to fall, collapse.

And she remembers.

∾

As he brings the knife up above her neck, she does a most curious thing: she rubs her face against the lilacs. The reverie of scent, after all, can make any animal, dead or undead, react in ways wholly unaccounted for.

"Pre .. tt .. y ..."

She pushes the syllables out as best she can. They are large and cumbersome in her mouth.

The knife falters and she does not hesitate.

In a movement so swift that he could not anticipate it, she shoves the lilacs into his face, bringing his skull down with a deafening crack on her gravestone, cleaving it messily in two.

His eyes swim with blood as she peels the flowers off his broken nose, licking the buds before shoving them clumsily into her mouth.

She leans in, and cradling her former lover's dripping head, she licks his lips and sighs. He never understood how much she loved lilacs.

HOW TO BRING YOUR DEAD LOVER BACK

Ask the man in the dark blue Chevy Impala to leave you at the second left after the crossroads. Crossroads are for devil-deals and demons and it's too late for that.

Take your backpack with you but leave your shoes in the car. You'll have to suffer, at least a little, to get where you need to go.

Walk along the desert-skirting road. Don't get hypnotized by the cactuses in bloom, their flaming headdresses swaying in the hazy air. Stay away from coyote tricksters; they'll smell the blood on your feet, gobble you up, leave your bones to bleach by moonlight.

In an hour, or maybe ten hours, a figure will approach. She'll look like a woman in her 40s with dirty blond hair and shimmering tattoos. Don't look at the tattoos, no matter how seductively they dance.

Talk to the woman, but don't tell her you've been looking for her. Death likes to think she's the only one who ever knows where she is.

When Death asks you back to her place, tell her you know a honky-tonk she'd like. Lead her down the road but always walk in front of her. Never let Death walk next to you, especially in the desert.

Buy Death a bottle of tequila when you get to the honkytonk. Don't drink a drop, no matter how nicely she offers. She'll try to cheat you by passing out, saying she's too drunk but one should never believe Death. Make sure she drinks the entire bottle before the moon rises.

After the last drop leaves the bottle, tell Death that you've found her, led her to drink and comfort and now she owes you a favor. Don't flinch while you say this or it won't work.

Make Death promise to let me go. Promise anything.

When Death agrees, I will appear behind you. Don't turn around. Everything will go to hell if you turn around.

Once outside, open your bag and drop stale packs of Camels behind you, like breadcrumbs, so Death can't follow us.

Walk back toward the crossroads, make a deal with no one but get in the first car that comes by. Be patient. Don't look behind you.

Offer the driver whatever you have left of the stale cigs. When you find a diner at least 61 miles away, ask the driver to stop.

Look in the rearview mirror. I'll be there.

Eat as much as you can at the diner.

We have a long journey ahead.

IMPOSSIBLE WOLVES

He was a beautiful wolf. Not like the snow before it hits the ground, perfect and new, but sooty and grey like the snow that fell on this city once, that still falls in the Alt Stadt. He was not like the wolves from Mutti's stories: weedy things said to hang about your doorstep in midwinter, so insane with hunger they'd gnaw their own paws for blood. Who knows if that was ever true? Even if Mutti's stories lived on in the Alt Stadt, I couldn't believe in them here. There was too much hope in any tale that promised rescue, a prince, a trail of breadcrumbs leading back home.

He found me deep in the bramble behind the old synagogue that sat on the Elbe. The river was like a spine that split the Neue and Alt Stadts. The windows that were unevenly spattered on the flat face of the temple did not blink in the grey light. I was seeking tansy and blue cohosh for the girl's tea, herbs that only grow in the wild, that suffocate in the air of the regulated rooftop forests in the Neue Stadt. Wolves, some books say, are actually very shy creatures, but he held my eyes in his, his head cocked to the left, considering me, a new animal, perhaps. Or a predator.

I couldn't help but wonder if Mutti had sent him to me from wherever she was now, and if she did, why. To prove that the stories were true? What did that matter to me now that she was gone? As I stood and reached my hand out to the still creature (perhaps he was a hallucination, perhaps he couldn't be touched), I heard a muffled yell and the pop of a gun. It was not a sharp sound, but dense, a cloud of noise entering me and enveloping my brain like a cloak. Not at all like the shots Mutti described from the war. By the time the guard grabbed my arms and shook me out of my reverie, the wolf was long gone.

"What's wrong with you? Alone in a place like this! Coming to the border is dangerous, don't you know that?"

The authorities maintain that the Alt Stadt is crumbling and dangerous, and of course it is. But we cannot simply pave it over and pretend it doesn't exist. I did not care for it, not after Mutti, but the edges at least, were necessary, were home. I wanted to tell the guard these things, but words slid out of my mouth like melting snow and I ran home, my search for the herbs forgotten, my mind full of impossible wolves.

I do not know why I was so surprised. Mutti always said: the wolves will return. After being slaughtered and hunted nearly to extinction, pushed into the dark forests of Poland, *Canus lupus* would be seen again. I was sure, now that I thought of it, I had read about them in the papers, skirting the fields a long way from the stadts, stealing chickens, being mistaken for shadows in the night. A curious and triumphant threat. I had no idea why I'd tried to touch him; he was a dangerous animal, not a story.

I barely left the flat. The search for the girl's tea forgotten, I poured over Mutti's books, her maps of the cities, trying to figure out where the wolf was going, though why this obsession possessed me, I could not have said at the time. When you are lonely, you are compelled to do many things. He ran through my mind all day, spent the night in my dreams. In one, I got out of bed and walked through rooms, so many bare, bright rooms and the wolf, he was beside me, not a threat or even a protector, but a companion. This was very strange and yet not strange at all. Finally a door opened to a forest room heavy with trees, their branches laden with briar and rose. The floor was thick with green grass and everywhere were plants and flowers and a vast beaming light hovered somewhere above our heads, not quite reaching through the canopy. The wolf hung his great head and tears dripped down from his dark eyes. He was draped with garlands of laurel and his fur was curled back. He had many wounds but if they hurt him, he disguised it well. When we finally found a spot of sun through the briared branches, he lay down in the grass and slept.

A scratching at the door woke me. The cat had been out night-hunting, no doubt, and wanted a warm saucer of milk for her spoils. I have always been soft when it comes to animals.

"You stupid cat, why are you still out at this hour?"

The cat streaked in, a bolt of hissing grey. She stopped behind the large table that lay between the courtyard door and my bedroom and seeming to gather herself, stalked closer and closer to the darkness she'd come from, growling all the way.

The only thing waiting outside was a rough bundle of tansy, covered in the dirt of barren fields, the scent of dirty snow.

~

No one had ever looked upon me with such lust. I knew what he wanted and at the thought my ribs tightened and my belly clenched with a hunger that I had never before considered, let alone felt.

"Ja?" I gripped the hard syllable with my tongue. I needed to get ahold of something, anything before I clawed at this stranger until I reached his skin.

"Frau, I need a poultice for my sister."

His eyes were dark, bottomless even. I could not find anything in them, neither lies nor the truth, yet they were familiar.

I could not answer, and so he continued.

"She is with child. Her labor will be … a difficult one. All her others have been. We need to make the child come in the next week or we are afraid …"

"You will lose both." I finished, finding myself. "However, I do not know why you come to me. I, as I am sure you know, end life in the womb. I am not a midwife. That was my mother."

"Surely you must know, must have some knowledge, however … old." He cocked his head then. "This is what I have heard … this is what the stories say."

His eyes begged me to fall into them, bowls of night sky in his face, so hungry, so hungry. And when he closed them only then did I come forward into his reach. Only then did I lean into his mouth. His lips were sweet grass and herbs, strong as if he had been holding their pungent smell bundled in his mouth. Only his lips touched me but he began to shake and shake and shake, a tree giving up its last leaves for winter.

In some sense I knew what was happening, but I was not afraid. How could I be when he was here with me? It was like one of Mutti's stories, one of her patients from the old war, only instead of a sad fairy tale covered in dust, he was here, alive, with me.

And then we were as bare as the sky and when his smooth, lean body began to grow soft and sooty grey and I felt his tail slide up the back of my thigh, I found I did not care.

~

I woke to him, curled around my back, his mouth whispering something in a language I did not know. We were spread like stars over the dark kitchen floor, the sturdy wooden work table overturned and split in three uneven pieces.

"I have broken it."

I turned my head. He was looking into me, like he could see the way my veins twisted around my bones, like he was trying to puzzle them apart. He looked wan, his skin pale as river stones.

"You must eat. And then ..."

His eyes widened, holding me.

"I have something for you."

His grin was a crack in his face.

I moved around the kitchen and he watched me, picking this from a jar, plucking that from a bundle suspended from the rafter to dry. I did not need to consult Mutti's books, her many books. I knew what to do. I supposed I had always known, known it all. And when I finished, he was himself again, a field of soft grey on his back. He nuzzled my bare thigh and I placed the poultice in his open mouth. I supposed I would not see him again. But that did not make me sad.

The dawn air rubbed against my shins as he slunk out the door. Behind me the cat growled from her perch atop the cabinets. I did not expect her to understand. I threw my shift on and slipped my tall boots over my legs. I would walk along the edges of the river and find the blue cohosh for the girl's tea. I would look out for wolves and nightmares. I would not be afraid.

∾

The girl was grateful for the tisane. She asked to stay. She could not take care of this at the flat. Her boyfriend, his mother, they were at work at the disco, but they would certainly know, certainly pity her, encourage her to forget when what she needed was to remember, to know her story. The specks of blue were bright in her eyes, like berries. She looked into her steaming mug.

"I cannot handle their stares, their eyes blank as … paper moons, blending into their faces as if there were nothing inside them." She drank the tea down and, grimacing at the taste, asked: "Are you alone here?"

"Sometimes." I looked at her then, her pale, bright-specked eyes, the whiteness of her hair. I wondered why she would confess fear at the table of a stranger, here in this city of forgetting, where magic no longer existed and everyone was bright and happy.

"Women are always alone. We are only ourselves when we are alone; we become something, someone else when we are together and something else when we are with men and children. Being alone, remembering who you are ... it is not a thing to fear." Her face was soft then, like down.

"But you get ... visitors."

She looked at my books and the picture of Mutti I'd brought out from the cupboard, my cat snoring on the sill.

"You are not really alone."

She looked at me then, and nodded, as if sitting at my table for one moment of her life could help her understand. Then again, perhaps she did. Perhaps that was why she was here.

PUSH WITH ALL
YOUR LOVE

L isten, the first time you fly is unlike anything else—it is falling so fast the air burns your cheeks and it is the tight knot in your chest because you do not yet trust the air to hold you, because you do not yet know that now it is only up to you to save yourself. You do not yet understand your wings, black and webbed, bursting through your thin winter coat. The membranes of your new skin are too thin, you think, because you don't know it as the strongest part of you, nor do you understand how to love this new part of yourself. You still hold the past in your hands, unable to let it drop from the sky.

~

I knew our father meant to feed us to the Spirit. He sputtered round and round for days, spitting Gospel backwards, bloodying his fists against the walls. Mother had hidden all the guns, the knives, forgetting that one doesn't need weapons to kill, not when there are arms to twine and teeth to tear flesh.

We were alone in that dark country. And even if anyone could have helped, Mother was too proud to have allowed it. We licked rancid butter from our own dirty fingers when there was no bread and watched as she butchered our milk cow, Delilah, rather than beg meat from the neighbors.

Father sat in a corner licking fly paper, picking pests off the tacky strip and grinding them between his broken teeth, ignorant to any hunger but his own. The worst that our father had done was to not try to kill us. His mercy was never that kind, not until, of course, the Spirit possessed him. Then he stopped defiling us, and was concerned only with abusing his own body, pressing his pocket blade into his skin until the words of his master covered his flesh. I was not fooled. His violence would not taper. How could it when that was all he was made of?

I followed him into the woods that day, not because I gave up protecting myself, protecting us, but because I made up my mind to kill him. The rage in my blood had boiled so long, I could not distinguish it from the rest of me. It grew blacker, harder, as if one morning I would wake to find it twisting from my bones like thorns.

We trekked for hours. He sang the backward psalms of his Spirit and spun us in circles, hoping, I think, to disorient me enough so that if I ran, I would never reach home again, that I would perish of starvation, animal attack, exposure. Yet how could these kill me when they hadn't already? We climbed to the caves, loose dirt rivering around our feet in currents as we pushed higher up the slopes. He panted and sweat steamed off him like he was already on fire but with each step, my body grew lighter, as if I floated on an ocean, a sea of blue (though my body had never seen such a sea).

When we reached the hole, neither of us said a word.

Falling was almost the most beautiful thing I had ever felt. My body was so light—even the cracking of my bones did not feel bad. And when my flesh split open and the blood left it in a great rush, a sigh descended over me, a relief, a balm. I was cushioned on blackness, not the loam or mud at the bottom of the pit, but a web, hard yet buoyant that grew from my arms, that burst through the worn wool of my coat until the cloth rent and fell like an apron over my shoulders.

How did these wings feel? Hidden for so long yet new, they were part of me; they fit me and felt like they had been with me forever. I discerned no suture, felt no strange or cumbersome new appendage— they were as mine as were my legs and breasts and head. But the wings belonged to me yet more, having come only from me, having never been touched by another's hand.

I did not get to marvel at their unfolding, their flap and glide, not yet. I knew what I must do, knew that only I could save my sisters. We would wing and soar later, later, when we were together.

Back at the farm, our father was easily done. The Spirit abandoned him the moment he stepped off the chair, and as his bowels released and shins twitched the last of his life out, his eyes were remorseless brown flecks. I let him swing. In a moment he was joined by our mother, who did not cry for him, or for herself.

The fear, the love that lived in my sisters' eyes was broken, aggregated as a likeness in a shattered mirror. I wished I could carry you all away at once, though I never promised you that. You would never have believed it.

Instead I dressed you, my next youngest sister, in an old coat of mine, one that had seemed too big only days before, so much, if you remember, we stuffed the elbows and shoulders with straw. You seemed to have grown since our father led me away, your spine straightened, your eyes calm, light. I kissed your mouth and took your hands and led you away. The currents of dirt continued to flow down the hills we climbed together and with each step, the air seemed to whisper in our ears, songs of country death and life.

And when we reached the hole, I pushed with all my love. I did not wait for you to soar up, to ascend through the pines into the sea of blue sky, though I knew that you would. We had other sisters to attend to, after all.

WHAT'S ALREADY DEAD

You can't kill what's already dead. It's the only thing that's kept me alive all these years.

I was tiny, pale, so small that my mother thought drowning me in the bath (my first memory) would be easy, the best way to rid herself of a child by a man she hated, a man who'd treated her like an open womb, her only job to carry out his freakish legacy. All her other children had died in infancy, experiments in life that failed. Imagine her surprise when, after I had seemed to sleep like seaweed beneath tepid bath water, my eyes popped open like daisies and I burbled, "Mama?"

It's still hard to breathe under all that water. Every time Bash pushes me under and locks the top of my tank, my mind forgets. I panic. And then my body remembers. Bash says the crowd likes to see me flail. They like to know that their heroine is struggling. They've paid for a show after all.

When I was young, my mother tried other ways of getting rid of me. Driving a sewing needle into my neck, choking me with apples or poison wine. It was a sort of game. The stories you hear, rasps from the deformed throats of our neighbors in the sideshow, they always said she was my stepmother. Even they, who know little of normal families, don't like the idea of a mother making her own child scream. People always got the story wrong.

"How much can she take, ladies and gentlemen? How much pressure can her lungs take?" Bash has always been a bit of a showman. Not flashy enough for the big ring but still, something to keep the rubes in our small tent occupied while they wait for my body to go limp.

The tank had been my father's idea. In those days, his freak breeding act wasn't bringing in the bucks like he'd hoped, especially since his wife kept killing the twisted refuse from her womb. The rumors of the murderous mother and the unkillable spawn had circulated heavily around the bone yard. What my body could take was already an act. Father'd make a mint off rubes who'd want to see someone almost die over and over. Why spend your communion dollars hearing about the resurrection of an untouchable holy man through the garbled sing-song of drunken monks when you could actually watch a beautiful young thing drown and miraculously not die, hear the slap of her palms against the glass tank, for the price of popcorn?

"Her brain cells are beginning to expire. Soon, ladies and gentlemen, serious brain damage will begin to occur, transforming our lovely lady into a soggy bag of skin and bone." Bash knows how long it takes for the brain to shut down without oxygen, how long it takes for the lungs to burst with need, for the heart to explode. Even if those rules don't apply to me, he knows what it takes to damage the human body beyond repair.

By the time I was thirteen, Father was afraid Mama'd figure out a way to kill me for good, that she'd shut me in the tank overnight with a rock on the lid. My arms never were that strong, even if something else in me was. Mostly, though, I think he was afraid of losing his bleeder, and what Mama'd do to him if she wasn't focused on draining the rest of my life away. Truthfully, I should have been more afraid of him; Mama's womb had long since dried up and if anything happened to me, he'd be out a money-maker. But it was all I could do to survive her and still dream of arms that wouldn't strangle and teeth that wouldn't bite. You'd think there'd only be so many times that someone who is supposed to love you can bleed you out before you cease believing that someday they'll decide to love you back, that the stabbing in your heart will end.

Later, when the water is drained from the tank and the rubes have gone home and the lights of the midway are the only whiteness haunting the boneyard and Bash, sweet, cutting Bash, touches me, tries to sooth the hole in my chest, pluck the bones holding me together, I want to cry out, want to feel the release of myself, of what I was, and I want to give him more than even that, want to be more than that, for him. It was Bash that found me after they'd both finally had their way with me: he brought me back from that twilit place where the dead-brained live, that place between life and not really life. His touch made me live. Even so, it's hard to give him any idea of what I feel when he touches me, no matter how much I want to give it. But I can't be more than shuddering and silent.

After years of concentrating her rage on my neck, my wrists, my lungs and liver, Mama finally tried my heart, cutting it out with an old hunting knife. She wanted it done so bad, she didn't even bother to shut me into the tank, throw an old horse blanket over my face. My eyes were still as I watched. I felt her shake my heart in a bag of salt, the granules prickling the torn flesh before she pierced it with long tent stake, and held it over the cook pit before pressing it into the center of the flame. The tongue of heat burned me and the smoke filled my empty chest but I couldn't scream. I didn't have anything left, couldn't push my voice out of its damaged hole.

After eating what he thought was a charred swine, Father found me slumped against the tank, chest open, barely breathing but there. He panicked, I think. Wanting to save his act got caught up in saving his genetic line. He forgot to see that I wasn't really dead, or forgot to care. Maybe he thought to reanimate me, like a corpse, dead-alive and crazy to do his bidding. Maybe he wanted to make me kill his wife, make me frighten the other freaks, the other carnies who started to look askance, get nervous when the act became too real, when his wife, my mother, started climbing in the tank with me, not just holding me down but strangling, cutting with her long sharp nails until ribbons of blood snaked into the water, making it a sick pink. Whatever his reason, his fingers jolted me like iron and his mouth tasted of my heart.

Father hadn't counted on Bash. Hadn't counted on him fingering the blood roses of strangulation on my neck, kissing them numb. Tucking my head beneath his, his wiry arms tight around my bruised and bloated skin. Humming me to sleep and laying me on a bed of sparkle-feathers from the discarded costumes of the acrobats in the next trailer over. Holding chloroform, strong enough to take down wiry tigers and sad elephants, over my father and mother's mouths, finding an old quarry so deep in the middle of woods haunted by thieves and madmen. He woke me with a grin that morning, with eyes burning with something I can only call love, the only love I've ever felt, and he held my hand as I pushed their weighted bodies down, down, down, where they'd wake up, where they'd scream, where they'd never come back.

BIRTH RITUAL

A woman who loves a woman is forever young

—Anne Sexton

I thought of rubbing your skin with saffron, so when you woke up, you'd be of sunny disposition. But then I thought, where can I get saffron? And in the middle of the Black Woods? So I settled on ash and moon water and that was that."

"Did I cry?"

"You looked upon me with eyes as quiet as stone and I knew you were mine."

My mother loves to tell me how I was born. I suppose all mothers do. Of course, she's not my real mother. My real mother is dead. Or probably dead.

She's my second mother. The second mother, my mother tells me, is the true mother. The one that chooses you, the one that wants you, more than anything, the one that makes the sacrifice to keep you. My true mother found me, she says, wrapped in a cabbage sack, cold, so cold and far from the hearth fire of my real mother. Then she made me warm again.

"And now, my darkling dove, more tea, I believe." She shakes her clay mug in my direction and I sift more tea into the pot and set the water to boil. Peering out the cloudy glass of the kitchen window, I see a hawk. It calls as it soars into a warm updraft and soon it is so small, a red-brown dot in the darkening sky. I believe its body must have disappeared, to be so far from the ground.

~

She taps the wooden table with her long pale fingernail, opaque as almond meat, and the steam clouds her face, rimming her black eyelashes in garlands of condensation. I slip my own slim fingers into a corner of my blue handkerchief and gently press her cheeks dry. Little things like this are the least I can do. She is such a doting mother. Indeed, she has more than kept me safe: she has taught me how to love. And even when I am ungrateful and unforgiving, when I shrug away her caresses, she still loves me. I am her best companion, she says. And she is my anchor.

"Why don't you read my leaves, my dear?" She squints, her look happy and sharp, like a cat staring into a pool of sunlight. She's been trying to teach me her ways, her art, to see futures in the soppy dregs of her tea. I can make shapes, sometimes tell yesterday's weather. It is hard, she says, to know what is to come from what has been. I've begun to see other things reflected in windows, puddles, the well water, anything in which I would normally see myself, smiling at her side. There are no mirrors in our house. If there were, I believe I would see in them, too.

Lately, I see a man. His teeth and fingernails are red, his smile hungry, devouring. I recognize him from pictures in books, stories, and dreams my mother has of her old life, before I was born. I am careful not to mention him, or the life she came from; the people outside our little forested world, she says, are cruel. No one else is allowed inside our love. It is perfect the way it is.

Tipping my eyes into her cup, I make out three lumpy shapes. One of them has strands of blue cornflower across its dark body, like a streak of flowers in a field of night. Another's face is masked with rosehips, sodden rosehips. The other is more formless, colorless, though it seems to be inching up the side of the cup. Climbing almost.

"It will be stormy and the rains will last for ... three days."

"Are you certain?" Mother squints at the clear sky and I remember how she used to punish me for lying, for pushing her away with untruth, for questioning her love for me.

"Well, as certain as I ever am."

I tip the tea leaves into the soil below the open window, unnerved at my lies, her easy acceptance of them, the man. Perhaps if I keep denying his presence, I can make him disappear. I must keep my mother to myself. She is all I have.

"How about a walk? You must move your body or it will rust."

Mother smiles at the old tin-woodsman joke, a relic from the many stories she filled my mind with as a child. Though she raised me up all these years, my mother is still young.

"If it will be as you say, I don't believe you will be out there very long."

She lets the line linger in the air like a question, a breath that sits in the belly of a dying man, waiting to be exhaled.

"And I must rest. You will find, when you are older, that having a daughter takes quite a lot out of you."

I laugh. We both know I will never have need of a daughter, not when I have a true mother. All I want and have is to be hers.

"I will be back soon."

I tuck my hair into a pale yellow cap and she replies: "Yes, soon."

～

We are alone here. We always have been. The world is a lonely place for a woman and a child. We've always only had each other. I suppose we always will. The woods stretch in every direction and beyond, to the north, is a frozen ocean, though I have never seen it.

My mother has never been well and a long journey would be beyond her. Sometimes I see the shores of this ocean, sometimes they crash against the backs of my eyelids and rush into my ears while I sleep. Sometimes I wake and feel the swells of the waves in my chest. Sometimes I think it will suffocate me, this ocean I've never seen. Sometimes I have to walk, to the high rock and beyond, where the brambles grow and grow and only then can I turn back to our house, to sleep.

A cry above me reminds me that I am not in dreams now, but awake, and my eyes follow the hawk as she sits in the top of a tree. She's calling to no one, I think, until I see a flat brown dot getting closer and closer until, there he is, beautiful and soaring, his wings stretched so much larger than I will ever be. The female hawk fluffs herself large and squawks as he alights on her branch. She looks as if she is about to strike him with her talons for getting too close.

I have never touched anyone except my mother. I wonder if that is what the female is thinking now, as her suitor encroaches on her. And I wonder what that must be like, to be faced with what most stories say is inevitable. Stories do not understand the love between a true mother and her daughter, I think.

It is only then that I notice that the birds have flown. As if realizing they had an audience. I pick stones and throw them into the bramble field, collect the tiny, hard spikes that have fallen below the hedges. If I put them in a tin, I can shake them at magpies, startle them away from Mother's garden. I am careful not to touch their barbs, not to lean too close to the hedges as I collect the thorns at their feet. Would I bleed if their long, sharp arms wrapped around my shoulders, my legs? Who would free me if I were to become tangled?

~

"I used to be young, so young. And beautiful. You'll never know how beautiful." My mother rocks in her chair by the window, a useless cat in her lap, staring through cloudy glass into the nothing world outside our house. She's been distracted these past days, forgetting our lessons, drifting off in the middle of a favorite story.

"You are beautiful, Mother. And powerful. You created me. And I'll never leave you."

When Mother gets in one of her melancholic states, I remind her of these things, I comfort her. And soon she recovers herself, her sharp wit, her voluminous laugh. And then she says:

"Oh, turtledove liver, did I ever tell you of the time I tricked the constable's wife into giving me her fattened goose? Slipped a bit of herbal suggestion into her tea and smeared a gob of raven fat on her knitting needles. Oh, it was quite a time, I'll tell you now. Cat and I ate goose for a month, didn't we, you old moggie, eh?" And she throws that old cat a marrow bone she's been saving for our soup.

But today, today she simply stares. Whispers: "Am I? Am I?"

∿

I fill the corrugated tub. Sprinkle lavender and verbena in the warm water and help Mother out of her robes. I remember our baths when I was younger, smaller. When she would run a cloth over my skin and kiss my newly clean shoulders and wrists and neck and teach me how the love between mother and daughter was so special, so special. Nothing can ever come between it.

We haven't been able to fit in the tub for some time and though we take our baths separately, I am always there to comfort her if she needs me. What else is a daughter for but to comfort her mother?

I hear a bird tapping at the glass with its hard beak while I wash her. And again as I spread salve over her skin until it is soft as a wing. I wish the horrid cat would eat the bird or at least frighten it away before it startles Mother. She is so tired, and for the first time, her eyes seem older, as if she has aged years in the space of a few days of sadness. I do not understand why she is so sad, why she pushes away my kisses, stares out the windows, just stares, as if there is something out there that is greater than what she already has. How do I make her forget her yearning, forget everything but my arms?

∿

I walk for miles, my arms full of flowers, sweet grasses, delicate herbs, even a robin's nest or two. I'm not sure what I am going to do with it all. But I will create something wonderful and magical. Something to wake mother out of her melancholy.

Upon reaching home, I am intent on hiding my spoils. I store them in the basement cupboard, the one with the lock and the shelf large enough for a child who won't obey. The stairs back up to the kitchen are narrow and long, closed in by the drying herbs that dangle from the rafters above, the cloying aroma of valerian and skullcap cloaking the scents of tea brewing or meat stewing.

So it is more than a shock to open the door and be assaulted by the odors of dirt and leather, pine and grass and ocean. There is no mirror, no window or scrying pot. But there is a man. And there is Mother. A moving picture begins to dance before my eyes: legs and hands jerk and crawl over each other like spider legs, two mouths gasp apart and press together, gasp apart and press together, first my mother's beautiful, pale, soft mouth, and then a younger, pinker set of lips, a red tongue darting. And oh, but it isn't mine. It isn't mine.

∿

"You must be the daughter. You are quite as beautiful as your mother tells."

He speaks and all I can see is his mouth, so red, so dark. Almost bloody. What could my mother want with that mouth? He speaks again but I am cloaked in his odors: damp earth, broken hide, soaring branches, and salt air. I can only see his mouth. My mother's voice bleeding at the edges of the room. Her body so flushed, like his bloody mouth, reaching again for him, for me.

~

Only days later, my mother is no longer young. Sunken pitted eyes, rotting skin stretched over bones that poke through at the fingers and toes and elbows, blood dripping from the chin: my true mother is being devoured by the man. I am no longer her lover, love, beloved. She is a walking corpse, everyday grabbing at the younger meat at her table, but she is drowning, drowning in her lust for him and he takes and takes and does not comfort or care for her. He does not love her.

When they finally collapse from their lust, I make a clarifying salve, mix it with my own blood (it's hers, it's hers, it will always be hers), and spread it over her eyes, her lips, her belly. She will come to me, she will have to, my blood will compel her and we will leave this man, this place, I will take my mother on my back, take her to the frozen ocean and we will walk across, find a new, cold home. Only for us, only for us.

The old cat sits on Mother's chest and I set to work on the man. Carefully, so carefully, I start with his mouth: each thorn from the bramble bushes punctures his skin easily, as if, inside, he were made of butter or feathers. He will not wake, not yet. I slipped enough valerian into their whiskey cups that they will both sleep for hours yet.

I stick the spikes around his eye sockets, his nostrils and jaw and start a line that bisects him: down neck and chest, sticking one deep, deep in his navel. I watch the blood pool there for a moment, mesmerized by the ruby color of it. Perhaps this is what my mother was so taken by? Jeweled blood that flows and pools endlessly? No, not endlessly, everything ends, yes, everything must run out sometime, even in the stories.

When I am finished, there are thousands of barbs planted in his skin, a field of blood and pain, though he has not yet begun to wake.

~

In sleep, the princess is always cold and beautiful. She waits and dreams until her savior awakens her with a kiss. My mother, oh my true love mother, she is still skin-torn, and blood-tipped and oh, I kiss her and I kiss her, her brow, her lips, her shoulders, and belly and thighs and everywhere and everything she ever did to love me but she is still cold and rotting and she does not wake.

The cat has moved to my own lap and when she purrs I think of all the things I have done in my life. I have done everything my mother asked, even when I was cross and uncooperative and unloving because I did not know better. I tried to keep her young with my love, but we are too exposed here if hawks can fly. And if dreams and pools are full of reflections, they are not dark enough.

Her bones are sighing as her flesh settles into them, all the love she once gave me, eaten by the man, now gone from her body, all her blood, tears, drained away. She folds in on herself: knees to chest, palms to shoulders. She cradles her bones as if she will rock herself to sleep. She is only dust now. Oh, only dust, and how will I survive without her love? As I take her folded body, so light, like a bundle of leaves, of grass, of herb, the man is beginning to stir. I leave him to wake to himself.

~

Mother lies on the cupboard shelf, sleeping mummy-doll. I know she will feel safer if I shut the cupboard door and lock it. I always have. I know the sweet herbs I garlanded round her head and neck will comfort her as will the soft swaying of the dark herbs over the stairs on a windy night.

I do not need much, I think. Mother always said: ash and moon water. I will bring sweet grasses and thorn, for my daughter will need to be harder, sweeter, more resilient and better than I was. But first, I will need saffron, perhaps away across the frozen ocean I will find it.

The cat rubs my shins and growls a bit as we stand in the yard, hawks circling, landing too close for her liking. They are beautiful creatures. I never noticed before; their feathers more than just brown, but mottled with every shade of red and grey and even deep blue.

One leaves me a tail feather as she pokes her head through the open bedroom window. And as the screams begin, I think, what a gift. What ruthless love my daughter will have.

PUBLICATION ACKNOWLEDGEMENTS

"The Dark Valley of Your Lungs" was published under the title "The Cult of Death" in *Shimmer Zine*, 2015

"Pripyat" was published in *The Golden Key*, 2014

"The Children's House" was published in *The Drum Literary Magazine*, 2016

"Hansel and Gretel" was published in *The Medulla Review*, 2011

"The Child of Midwinter Eve" was published in the *Winter Animals Anthology: Stories to Benefit PROTECT*, 2013

"Our Courtship, Our Romance" was published in *Femme Fatale* under the name Zoe More, 2012

"How To Bring Your Dead Lover Back" was published in *Mythic Delirium*, 2013

"Impossible Wolves" was published as a chapbook by Deathless Press, 2013

"Push With All Your Love" was published by *The Golden Key*, 2014

"What's Already Dead" was published under the title "The Unkillable Girl" by *Innsmouth Magazine*, 2013

"The New Heroes at the Old Fairgrounds" was published in *Protectors 2: Stories to Benefit Protect*, 2015

ACKNOWLEDGEMENTS

I'm so grateful to you, dear reader, for spending time with my stories. Thanks to each and every person who has read my words; I hope they've changed you and challenged you, even in a small way.

It truly takes a community to build a book, and I could not be more thankful for mine. There is one person, however, who is the reason you are holding these stories in your hands, my editor and tireless book midwife, Katie Eelman. Katie's faith in me and my work, her endless energy, enthusiasm, positive attitude, humor, and encouragement has buoyed me throughout this process. She has been so much more than my editor; she has been my promotions and marketing guru, publicist, and tireless advocate. Nothing I could write could adequately thank her for all that she has done and continues to do, so I'll just say that she is a blessing that I am grateful for every day.

Thank you, Stacey Dyer, for the most incredible cover of all time. Huge buckets of unicorn tears go to Anna Cassell, whose interior illustrations are amazing and will soon be tattooed all over my body.

I'm also eternally grateful for the writers, artists, teachers, and just plain amazing people I was privileged to know and work with while constructing this book. I could not hope to name them all in this small space, so here are a few folks who were instrumental by offering me insight, encouragement, and fellowship while I was writing: Kat Good-Schiff, Suwada Hinds, Christopher Irvin, Jan Kozlowski, Sonya Larson, Blanca Lista, Bracken MacLeod, Liz Madden, Jess Mann, Rebekah Murphy, Errick Nunnally, Regie O'Hare Gibson, Nicole D. Pittman, Sophie Powell, Lauren Rheaume, Sue Williams, Jake Tavares, Toni Thayer, DBT, and Vicki Yuen. I'd also have been lost without my mentors, students, and colleagues at Bard College, Simmons College, Goddard College, GrubStreet, the Young Writers Conference at Champlain College, and the New England Horror Writers. I'm also hugely appreciative to my writing groups past and present: the Cajun Sushi Hamsters From Hell, and the Mad Dogs.

I'd also like to thank my extremely large family; if I named names we could be here for two hundred more pages, but suffice it say, I love you all.

Thanks, too, to Kate Layte and the Papercuts/Cutlass family.

I'm still in awe of the kind praise of Porochista Khakpour, Helen Marshall, Randy Susan Meyers, Irenosen Okojie, and Paul Tremblay. Thank you so much. I'm deeply appreciative of your incredible support.

Many thanks go to the publications in which some of these stories originally appeared.

Writers do not exist in vacuums, no matter how much we might wish it at times, and so I think it appropriate to thank the authors whose writing has most influenced and challenged me: Jorge Luis Borges, Octavia Butler, Angela Carter, Lucille Clifton, Neil Gaiman, Shirley Jackson, Kelly Link, Gabriel García Márquez, Maggie Nelson, Helen Oyeyemi, Sylvia Plath, Selah Saterstrom, Jeanette Winterson, and so many others. My work would not exist without yours. Thank you for being my literary ancestors and inspirations.

All the love to Bonnie and Leslie Adams, who allowed me to hang my hat with them and all our cats in the Pink House. It's the best place I've ever called home. I also have to thank all the kitties, some of whom have left us, some of whom still haunt the halls: Fritz, Cody, Zoe, Lola, and the ever handsome Bizarro.

I don't know what I would do without my best friend, Stephanie McColl. She is always there to cheerlead, mock lovingly, and take me to Canada. I'm looking forward to being an even crankier old lady with her in the years to come.

My stories and I could not be here without my amazing parents. My mother, Charlene Manchester Jorge, deserves all the thanks and hugs *this* big for reading to me endlessly, for buying me books, for teaching me to be number one on my absolute yes list (thanks, Oprah!), and for encouraging me to follow my dreams, even when the steps are uncertain. My father, Jose Viera Pereira gets all the credit for my love of the strange and the dark. Thank you, Jose, for teaching me that it's always important to unabashedly be who you are, especially if you are weird. Finally, big creepy thanks to my stepmother, Debra Pereira, for encouraging me to write my disturbing stories and who gave me tons of horror, thriller, and serial killer books when I was much too young.

And finally, to my babies, present and in the ether, Vinnie and The Mitten, the best familiars a crazy cat lady writer could ask for.